CLOSING TIME
AT THE
SUNNY-SIDE-UP

CLOSING TIME AT THE SUNNY-SIDE-UP

DAVID NIALL WILSON

2025

Published by **Shotgun Honey Books**

215 Loma Road
Charleston, WV 25314
www.ShotgunHoney.com

Photo by Ysbrand Cosijn.
Cover Design by Bad Fido.

Trade Paperback ISBN: 978-1-956957-83-9
Digital eBook ISBN: 978-1-956957-93-8

10 9 8 7 6 5 4 3 2 1   25 24 23 22 21 20

*This novel is dedicated to the old gang on Twitter,
when it didn't suck, and to S. A. Cosby,
who will appreciate the cars.*

CLOSING TIME
AT THE
SUNNY-SIDE-UP

ONE

The sun dipped toward the horizon, heading south toward Mexico. Sam West followed, kicking a worn leather boot down on the gas pedal of his gleaming black 1966 Ford Thunderbird and shooting gravel off the side of the deserted stretch of highway. Every mile or so, he glanced into the rearview, but the road behind and before him remained deserted.

He saw the brilliant lights of the Sunny-Side-Up Coffee Shop blazing in the distance. He focused on them. They meant he was close to coffee, a slice of Mort's pie, and Delilah. It was better than thinking about what he'd left behind. It was better than thinking about what was likely ahead for him if he didn't drive hard and fast. It was better than a lot of things. Mort made a hell of a pie, and Sam figured it was worth one last stop before he took a card from the Taco Bell dog's deck and made a run for the border.

He took the last few miles at around a hundred, letting the big 390 purr. He'd spent more years and money restoring the car than he had building his life. It showed on both. He was worn, and the T-Bird gleamed.

The parking lot was almost empty, as usual. There were never many customers at the Sunny-Side-Up. It was too far out of the nearest town to be anything but a stop on the way to somewhere else. There was an old, dusty Cadillac parked near the side door. That was Mort's. The lights illuminating the gas pumps were brilliant white. Bugs flitted around them. In contrast, what illumination leaked out through the dusty diner windows was yellow, like dirty sunlight.

Sam killed the engine and sat for a minute. He'd been coming to the Sunny-Side-Up every night for about six months. Every night he had coffee, pie, and an eyeful of Delilah. It was a place on the edge of forever, and that's how long it seemed he'd been there. Too long to stay in one place without really putting down roots. Too long to flirt with the same woman and never even take her out for a beer. Now it was likely too late.

The road glittered in the moonlight, stretching out beyond the coffee shop and on into the distance. Sam shifted to park, pulled the key out of the ignition, and slid the steering wheel to the right. It was one of the many things he loved about the old car. The steering wheel twisted toward the center of the dash to make it easier for the driver to get in and out. It was also convenient for turning the wide front seat into a bed.

The dashboard lights died, their strobed after-image like a panel on the bridge of a starship. The car had a black leather interior that matched the paint. It wasn't a stock color. When Sam bought it, it had been robin's egg blue. He liked to tell anyone who asked that he painted it because he didn't have any robin's egg blue boots to match, and it just seemed easier than shoe shopping. He liked talking about the car more than he liked talking about himself. He even liked it more than Mort's pie, but at that moment, it was close.

There were other useful things about the T-bird. The trunk was immense. It would have held a cow, or a motorcycle, or half a football team. Right now it held all he owned, and it was damned near empty. He took a final look back the way he'd come, then climbed out of the car and headed into the diner.

. . .

Delilah stood behind the yellowed Formica counter, counting, and recounting the five dollars and forty-five cents in tips in a chipped, Houston Oilers mug. She was just the irritating side of thirty, tall with dark hair and darker eyes. She wore her apron slung at an angle, like a gunslinger's belt, and her nametag rested right where most of her customers' conversational viewpoint stopped and started. She was pretty, but with hard cut lines that gave the impression if you touched her, you might get cut. Deep.

Behind her, flipping a burger on the greasy grill, Mort Templeton leered at her from behind. Mort was fifty-five and unapologetic about his lack of culture. He'd been running the diner since his early thirties, seen several presidents and a whole lot of crap flash across the screen of more cheap televisions than he could count (he wasn't real good with numbers), and he didn't give a fuck about anything but Mort. He drank himself to sleep at night, got up early and baked pies for fat-assed truckers, and he hired waitresses like Delilah because he liked watching their asses walk around the shop. Sometimes he took advantage of their situations if he could manage it. If not, he watched.

At one end of the counter, Stan Langston sat, sipping his coffee in silence. On the counter beside his coffee cup sat an old Zippo lighter. On the side was a rebel flag so faded that there were streaks of gun-metal gray running through the crossed stripes. An open pack of unfiltered Pall Mall's lay beside it; a recent resident dangled from his lip. Delilah had asked Stan once why he smoked Pall Malls, and the old guy had given her a toothless grin.

"Smokes're expensive, girl. Cain't afford to hand 'em out to ever'body who thinks they need one. You smoke these babies," he tapped the pack on the counter and extracted one almost lovingly, "and nobody even asks. Only desperate men and bums smoke Pall Malls."

Delilah didn't have to ask which side of that haystack Stan rolled off of.

When the bell above the door rang, and Sam walked in, they all glanced up. Delilah smiled. Mort nodded curtly. Stan sipped his coffee and went back to nursing his Pall Mall.

Sam West was a tall man. His jeans were black and straight, not skinny or dangling off his ass like a punk but worn and well fitted. He wore a black t-shirt and a black leather jacket. His wallet hung from a chain attached to his belt. His engineer boots were scuffed and worn, but, like the T-Bird outside, showed signs of polish and care. His hair was dark brown and tied back in a ponytail. He crossed the room to his usual booth by the window, where he could see the back fender of the T-bird through the window.

Delilah crossed the room slowly. She considered putting an extra sway in her step to see if she could get Sam to smile; then she caught the expression on his face and let it slide. She set an empty mug in front of him and poured strong, fresh black coffee into it slowly. Then she straightened and looked at him.

"Get some bad news?" she asked.

"You might say that," Sam said. He stared out into the night for a moment longer, then made some sort of inner decision and turned back.

"I killed a man last night," he said.

Delilah stared at him. She took half a step back, not shocked, but surprised.

"It's not like that," he said. "This guy really needed killing. No guilt here."

Delilah sat the coffee pot on the table, leaned on the edge, and frowned.

"Then what's the problem?"

"When I came home from the garage, the cops were all over my place. Had the street cordoned off with that damned yellow tape. I don't think I'll be going back in to work."

"No shit."

"Yeah. Guess I'm gonna have to get out of here tonight. It's a shame."

"A shame?" Delilah said. She smiled. "You kill a man, they start a manhunt, and that's it–it's a shame?"

"Not the killing," he said. "That part's fine. I guess I'm gonna miss you."

"So, you're leaving now?"

"I guess I am."

"Headed anywhere in particular?"

"South, I think, then west. I'm gonna hit Interstate 10 and head on toward California."

"Funny," Delilah said. "I always wanted to see California. You got any money?"

"Not much," he said. "I was kind of in a hurry."

Delilah turned and glanced over at where Mort was getting ready to slide the burger he'd been frying off the grill.

"You still have the gun?" she said.

Sam glanced up at her, looked for something in her eyes, and found it. He reached into the deep pocket of his leather jacket and pulled out a gleaming, chrome-plated .45. He laid it on the table.

"Of course," he said.

"Mind if I borrow it?"

Delilah didn't wait for his answer. She reached out, grabbed the gun, and lifted it easily.

"Don't smudge it," Sam said.

Delilah popped the clip out of the gun, checked the rounds, then slapped it back into place. She worked the action. Locked and loaded, the gun glittered in the smoky, yellow light.

"Five brothers," she said, catching a hint of surprise in Sam's expression.

She turned and headed back toward the counter. Stan saw her coming back, and called out to her.

"Hey, can a guy get a cup of coff–"

Delilah lifted the .45, aimed, and pulled the trigger. It caught the smoldering tip of the Pall Mall full on and blasted it back through Stan's face. The back of his head exploded, splashing blood, bone, and gristle across the faded Nascar photos taped to the cheap paneling at his back.

"Jesus," Sam said. He took a sip of coffee.

Delilah spun and aimed the gun at Mort. "Afraid I'm going to be checking out a little early tonight, Mort," she said. "I'll be taking some severance pay."

The short, balding cook backed away, glancing right, and left and trying to gauge his odds of dropping to the floor and getting the shotgun behind the cash register. Problem was, Delilah knew where the gun was.

"It's cool," Mort said. "You don't have to…"

"Sorry again, Mort," Delilah said. "I'm afraid I do."

She fired point blank into his face. Mort spun away and back. Bits of his skin and brains scattered out the back of his skull. Some of it arced through the air, almost like it was in slow motion, and fell onto the grill, where it started to sizzle. Delilah paid no attention to him. She went straight to the cash register, opened it, and emptied it into her purse. Then she leaned down and grabbed Mort's sawed off shotgun and a handful of shells. She tucked the ammo into her pockets and stood.

Outside, the grinding whine of an eighteen-wheeler pulling into the lot broke the sudden silence.

"We'd better go," Sam said. He took back the .45 and slipped it into his pocket.

Delilah nodded. Sam leaned over the counter and stared down at Mort. Then he reached into the tip jar on the counter, took out a quarter, and flipped it down onto the old man's bloody corpse.

"What was that for?" Delilah asked.

"He made one hell of a pie," Sam said. "No sense tempting karma."

Outside the hiss of hydraulic brakes sounded. Sam walked to the door and held it open as Delilah slipped out. They made their way around the side of the building to the T-bird and slid inside. Delilah tucked the shotgun under her seat.

"Shall we?" Sam asked.

She smiled and nodded. "What are you waiting for, cowboy? Let's ride."

TWO

Terence Bender crossed the brilliantly lit parking lot of the Sunny-Side-Up Coffee Shop slowly. He rolled his shoulders and squinted up at the bugs flitting around the lights. The place was dead. Almost no vehicles in the lot at all. He'd been driving for several hours, and though he was wide awake, his muscles were stiff. He had a couple of things in mind; coffee, and some of the pie he'd been hearing about for the last two hundred miles. Maybe a burger if they looked edible.

Terence was a big, broad-shouldered man with close-cropped hair just starting to gray at the sideburns. He had a full mustache, and an old ball cap so stained you couldn't make out the faded "Love it or Leave it" American flag patch on the front unless you were closer than most people got tilted back on his head. He wore a pair of sunglasses too dark for almost any occasion.

As he approached the door of the diner, he heard the rumble of an engine–an old, powerful V-8. He stepped up close to the building in case the driver didn't see him standing there and watched. A second later, a black T-bird shot out of the shadows, turned with a quick screech of tires, and roared onto the highway. Terence watched until the taillights faded into the distance, then turned, pushed the door open, and entered the diner.

The first thing he noticed was that something smelled bad. There was a sweet, acrid smoke coming from the area of the grill. Then he saw Stan, and the splatter of blood and flesh on the wall. Moving slowly, careful to touch nothing, he crossed the diner to the counter. He leaned over, saw Mort's body on the floor, and backed away.

He glanced at the glass display on the counter, still lined with freshly cut slices of pie, and he scowled. Terence turned back to the door and shook his head. He glanced back at the pie one last time.

"Damn," he said. He pushed through the door with enough force to shake the door in its frame and headed back across the parking lot.

* * *

Terence re-crossed the parking lot a lot faster than he had on the way in. A door had opened on the side of the eighteen wheeler's trailer. At the foot of the stairs his wife, Helen, Kurt Carter, a hefty kid in his late twenties, and Joe Mulak, a big man with a clean-shaven dome of a head and arms like small trees waited. They called Mulak "Mule" because he had a stubborn streak, and because when it came time to work, he could pull a hell of a load.

"What's up babe?" Helen called. "Where's the coffee?"

Terence glanced over his shoulder and shook his head again.

"About that," he said. "Someone better get back in there and get the professor. We got us a problem."

* * *

This time the four of them entered the coffee shop together. Terence held the door, then followed the others in. They all turned in a slow circle, taking in Stan's corpse, the blood, and the still smoking grill in silence.

"Jesus," Helen said. "What the hell happened here?"

"Offhand," Terence said, "I'd say someone didn't like the coffee."

Mule made his way around the counter and examined the rifled cash register, and Mort's collapsed form.

"Nope," he said, "That can't be it."

He leaned down and picked the quarter off of Mort's chest and flipped it through the air toward Terence, who caught it reflexively.

"They left a tip," Mule said.

"If you clowns are about done playing around," Helen said, "I think we'd better figure out what we're going to do before someone else shows up."

"Call the cops?" Kurt said. He didn't sound at all convinced.

"Sure," Terence said. "That's a great idea. Let's see, how would that go? We call them from out here in the middle of nowhere. They come, and they find us alone with two dead bodies, no one else around, and our fingerprints on the only actual bit of evidence. They ask what we're doing standing around in a coffee-shop full of corpses, and we say, sorry officers–we found 'em this way."

He flipped the quarter to Kurt.

"That," he added, "is a one heck of a stupid plan."

Kurt stared at the quarter in his hand, then wrinkled his nose and raised his head. "Okay," he said. "Bad idea. But what the hell is that smell?"

Mule glance at the grill and grinned.

"Brains and eggs," he said. "Light on the eggs…"

At that moment, the door to the coffee shop opened again, and Professor Gregory Verdino entered. Verdino was short, bespectacled, and as bald as Mule. He wore a khaki shirt and chinos, and he carried a tablet PC that he stared at right until the scent of Mort's brains grilling wafted across the room to him and caught his attention.

He glanced up and took the scene in quickly. He walked over to Stan, then around to where he could get a good look at Mort.

"Well," he said. "How fortunate."

The others turned and stared at him. Even Terence, who never showed the slightest surprise or emotion unless angered, let his jaw drop slightly.

"Fortunate?" Helen repeated slowly. "This is...fortunate?"

"Oh, absolutely," Verdino replied. "Very fortunate. I'm afraid we've got a lot of work to do, but at least there's coffee..."

Then, without a word to any of them, Professor Verdino walked across to the fuse box on the wall and, after fumbling with the switches for a few moments, managed to dim the outside lights, and drop the blinds over the windows. Satisfied, he went to the coffee shop door, and, with a quick and final gesture, he flipped the OPEN sign dangling in the doorway to closed.

▪ ▪ ▪

A few short hours later, the coffee shop was immaculate. Kurt and Mule, wearing white laboratory hazmat suits, mopped up the last of the cleaning chemicals and water. In the center of the floor, two cylindrical canisters, about four feet in height and two feet around, rested on a wheeled cart. Professor Verdino made a quick sweep of the place, nodded, and turned to the others.

"Grab some of that pie," he said. "We'll have to have it on the road. Fill up a couple of thermoses with coffee. We're about done here, and we need to get away before anyone else shows up. We can begin processing on the road."

Mule grabbed the handle of the cart. Kurt grabbed the

cleaning gear, and waited as Terence and Helen carried bags of food and the thermos bottles out the door. When everyone was clear, he ran his mop carefully over the floor where they'd just passed. The last thing he did was wipe any prints off the door with an antiseptic rag.

Then he hurried across the parking lot after the others and clambered up into the trailer. They closed the door, and a moment later, Terence rolled the big truck out from under the dimmed fluorescent lights and turned south.

THREE

The T-Bird was cruising easily at sixty-five, eating up the miles. Sam kept his eyes on the road ahead, scanning for Troopers hiding in the brush, and thinking. On the passenger-side seat, Delilah had kicked back. She had her shoes off, one foot up on the dash, the other tucked up under her. The silence wasn't tense, but it also wasn't comfortable. They'd gone from acquaintances with possibilities to road-partners on the lam in a very short period. Too short for lines to be drawn or conclusions to solidify. Finally, Sam broke the silence.

"Pretty harsh," he said.

Delilah turned to him, as if startled by the sound of his voice.

"Huh? What are you talking about?"

"Back at the coffee shop," he said. "Taking them all out like that–pretty harsh. Any chance you want to tell me what that was all about? I'd like to flatter myself and think you did it all for me, but…"

She studied him a moment, then turned back to face the road.

"I've been at that diner a long damn time," she said. "Too long. You've been through now, what, a couple of dozen times?"

"Something like that," Sam said.

"First time I saw that place, I was hitching across country. Thought I'd head out to California, see if I could break into the movies, or do some singing. Didn't have any money. Rode the last bit with a trucker named Ely. Ely was cool. He taught me every trucker song ever written and gave me beef jerky. I should have stayed in the truck. Instead, I got out at that coffee shop, and I met Mort."

"Mort…you mean the fry cook?"

"Mort the owner. Mort the douche bag. He told me it was, like, fate or something. He loses his best waitress, and there I come walking in through the door. Bastard. He started out lying and never slowed down."

"He didn't really lose a waitress?" Sam said.

"He lost her alright. Her name was Claire. Seems that she didn't want to sleep with his best customers, and that she thought she ought to have a room of her own. Since Mort disagreed, she hit the road."

"He treated you like that?" Sam asked. "He abused you?"

"You kidding? Not me. He tried. That guy in there taking the coffee intravenously? Stan? He helped. I stuck a fork through Stan's hand, and I told Mort he'd pay me on time and keep his hands off me, or I'd turn him in to the first State Trooper that came through the doors. When he said he didn't believe me, I twisted the fork. Stan convinced him."

"So, you had a sort of business arrangement."

"You might say that," she said. "It kept me alive and paid for a place to stay."

"So…if you had an agreement, I return to my original comment. Kinda harsh."

"My agreement didn't call for me giving any notice. And what are you, squeamish all of a sudden? Didn't you just kill a man? If I hadn't needed the job, I'd have done it a long time ago."

"Yeah, well, like I said, the guy needed killing. No choice."

"Let me ask you a question, cowboy," Delilah said. "You ever eat Mort's meatloaf?"

Sam glanced over at her, then nodded. "Once or twice. Pretty good, but not as good as the pie."

"You ever wonder why there's never any roadkill on that stretch of road?" she asked.

Sam was silent for a long moment, then he stomped on the gas and the T-bird shot ahead.

"You should have shot him in the balls."

FOUR

Well down Highway 281, headed south toward Mexico, Terence caught sight of a small dirt road headed off into the desert on their right. He slowed the rig, flipped on the signals, and made the turn as smoothly as possible. He knew that any serious jostling would bring Verdino or one of the others through the door into the cab yapping in his ear, and he wasn't in the mood for it. Bad enough they thought he should be able to take the rig four-wheeling whenever it suited them.

Helen sat beside him, sipping on a cup of coffee.

"You sure that's the right turn?" she asked.

Terence glanced over at her, and then back at the road. He didn't answer. They drove slowly off the dirt road into the desert. He drove until he couldn't see anything behind him but shadows, then he drove a little farther. A few moments later, the truck's lights winked out, and it disappeared into the wasteland as if it had never existed.

FIVE

The morning sun was already bright, glittering off the tiny bits of mica embedded in the highway. Officer James Goodman rolled down Highway 281, scanning the road ahead distractedly. Nothing much happened on this route, but that didn't mean he didn't need to pay attention – it was time for a pick-me-up. About a mile ahead, he saw the signs for a coffee shop coming into sight. He hadn't had breakfast, and the coffee in his thermos was barely tepid. As he approached, he slowed and pulled into the lot.

There was a single car visible, a beat-up Cadillac parked over by the door. There was no one at the gas pump, and when he got close enough to see the door clearly, he noted that the sign dangling in the window said "Closed".

He cruised through the parking lot. There was no one moving in or around the place, as far as he could see.

He parked and climbed out of his cruiser, taking his time, and keeping his eyes open. He moved slowly, but he was tense and ready. Something felt wrong, and though he didn't know what it was, he wasn't in the habit of ignoring gut feelings. If it felt wrong, he thought, it probably was, and if not, he lost nothing by being careful.

He peered in the windows, but could make out nothing in the dim, unlit interior of the coffee shop. He returned to his cruiser and grabbed the microphone of his radio.

"FOURSTARBASE, this is FOURSTARSIX, over," he said.

After a moment's hesitation, the radio crackled with static.

"FOURSTARSIX this is FOURSTARBASE. Copy."

"FOURSTARBASE, I'm parked out here at the Sunny-Side-Up Coffee Shop on State 281. Have we had any reports of anything strange out this way?"

"FOURSTARSIX, that's a negative. We haven't had anything this morning. It's been quiet."

"Copy FOURSTARBASE, that's the problem. It's a little too quiet here. I don't know exactly what the situation is yet, but you might want to get another car headed my way, just in case. I'll check it out, and I'll get back to you. Over."

"Copy, FOURSTARSIX. FOURSTARBASE out."

He replaced the microphone on its clip and turned back to the diner. He tried again to get a good look in through the window. It was coated with dust. He reached up to wipe some of it away and squinted.

The silence was broken by an ear-splitting BANG! Goodman jumped back, dropped to one knee, and drew his weapon.

"Jesus!" he said.

The echo of the backfire faded into the slow chugging of an ancient motor. Goodman turned and watched as a beat-up Ford pickup pulled slowly into the lot. It trailed white smoke and had more colors of paint on its doors and fenders than were sported by a rainbow. The driver spotted Goodman, slowed, and then stopped right in the middle of the parking lot. A moment later, the engine died reluctantly, spitting a final belch of smoke into the morning air.

An old man climbed down from the driver's seat. He slapped a dusty ball cap on his leg, arranged it atop his thin, gray hair, and crossed the lot to where Goodman stood, holstering his gun, and shaking his head.

"Morning, officer," the man said. "Something wrong? Mort ain't opened yet?"

"As a matter of fact, he hasn't," Goodman said. "The place is closed, and I don't see a sign of anyone inside. Who are you, exactly?"

"Grissom," the man said. "Merle Grissom, and happy to meet you officer. Funny about Mort, though. You say there's no one inside?"

Merle pointed over at the old Cadillac beside the building.

"That there piece of shit Caddy is Mort's–far as I know it's the only vehicle he's owned in the last twenty years. If he isn't here…"

"Someone took him out of here," Goodman said.

"Don't that beat all. I ain't seen this place closed but one morning for five years, and that was when Mort had the Whoopin' Cough."

Grissom started toward the door of the coffee shop.

"Guess we better get in there and see what happened to Mort."

"Wait," Goodman said. "What makes you think anything happened to Mort?"

Grissom glanced back at him, frowned, and shook his head. "Ain't you been listenin'?"

The old man pushed on the door to the diner. It swung open, unlocked. He entered without looking back. Cursing, Goodman followed. As he stepped through the door, he called out.

"Don't touch anything."

Inside, it was dark. Goodman crossed to the wall and flipped on the lights. He turned and scanned the room. Grissom was doing the same, shaking his head. The coffee shop was spotless. The tables and counter gleamed. The floor was mopped and buffed.

"Damn," Grissom said. "This ain't right."

Goodman glanced over at him.

"What 'ain't right' exactly?"

"This," Grissom said, swinging his arm in an arc to encompass the entire shop. "All of this. Mort never cleaned this place so good in all the years I've come here. You smell that?"

Goodman took a deep breath. "All I smell is floor cleaner."

"Exactly," Grissom said. "Never smelled anything like that in here before. Never. Mort cleaned up, he used ammonia. All he kept was Clorox–said it killed everything, and that shit reeked. This ain't it."

Goodman rounded the counter and stepped over to the grill. The grease had been cleared off the surface, and the bucket beneath had been emptied, but there was a scent of old oil and grease lingering.

"This hasn't been cleaned," he said.

Grissom whirled. "The grill? The Grill hasn't been cleaned?"

"That's what I said."

"I don't know what in hell happened here, officer, but I know what didn't. Mort didn't clean this place, and he would sooner have kicked his mama off a cliff than leave that grill dirty. Said it was his lifeblood, the only thing that mattered. He cleaned it every night with some kinda square stone–oiled it good. Something's not right." He glanced over at the counter. "That's funny too," he said.

"What's funny?" Goodman asked.

"That lighter. That belongs to Stan Langston. He hangs out here, talks to Mort and drinks free coffee all night. Never seen him without that lighter and a pack of Pall Malls. He wouldn't just leave that here."

"This Stan," Goodman said. "He drive?"

"Nope," Merle said. "Nope. Rides an old scooter. Thing barely gets fifteen miles per, but he's been patching it together since I can remember."

"I think it's about time you and I got out of here," Goodman said. "I have to call this in, and I think I'll need a crime scene unit out here."

"Don't suppose I could grab a soda for the road?" Merle said.

"Get on out of here before I run you in for questioning," Goodman growled.

Merle reached for the door, and Goodman stopped him.

"Wait," he said.

He pulled a flashlight off a loop on his belt and used it to work the latch on the door. Then he pushed it open gently and held it until Grissom was clear. He glanced over his shoulder at the coffee urn, frowned, and followed the old man out. It was looking like a very long morning, and he hadn't even gotten breakfast.

SIX

The old filling station Sam found was well off of the highway, tucked back at the end of a dusty, deserted road. About half the lights in the sign were out, and the pumps looked like something from a cable TV antique hunting show. The globes on their tops were lit, and as they pulled into the lot, a table came into view outside the office. There were three men seated around it, playing cards. They barely glanced up as the T-Bird rolled up to the pump.

Sam glanced over at them, and then at the pump.

"You think it's self-serve?" he said.

"I hope so," Delilah said. "If it's not, I think we'll be here a long time. You go ahead and fill up, I'm gonna see if they have anything to drink."

Sam killed the engine and in the ensuing silence, they both climbed out. The slamming of the T-Bird's doors echoed across the nearly empty lot. The men still didn't look up. Sam popped off the gas cap and grabbed the pump handle. The old machine thunked as it went live, and he pulled down the spring-loaded rear license plate holder, unscrewed the gas cap, and popped the nozzle into the spout. As gas began to flow, accompanied by the steady click of the old pump, Delilah turned and sauntered across the lot toward the office and the card game in progress. At her approach, the men finally glanced up.

One of the men tipped his chair back, then his hat, and looked Delilah up and down.

"Well," he said. "Look what we have here. Gen-u-ine travelers." The faded, soiled name tag sewn to his work shirt said 'Earl'.

Delilah stopped a few feet away. She smiled coyly.

"Anyplace a girl could get something cold to drink around here? It's hot out on that road."

"Kinda hot *here* about now," Earl said. He grinned, showing off half a mouth of yellow teeth. "Know what I mean?"

"You think so?" Delilah asked. She winked at him.

A pot-bellied guy with more beard than hair on his head and a nametag that read 'Jim Bob' nodded toward Sam and the T-Bird.

"That your husband?"

Delilah glanced back over her shoulder.

"Sam?" she said. "No, not my husband. He's more of an–acquaintance."

"There's a cooler inside," Earl said. "Help yourself. Sodas're a buck, beer's a buck fifty."

Delilah smiled. "Don't mind if I do," she said. She turned, waving her ass at them, and rounded the corner. A moment later the screech of the old office door opening brought Earl to his feet.

"Jim Bob, Bill, why don't you go see if you can help Mr. Sam 'sorta an acquaintance' on his way. I'm gonna go inside and see what I can do for the lady."

At the pump, Sam glanced up and noticed Delilah disappearing inside the office. When he saw Earl follow, he kept his head down and pretended he hadn't noticed. As Jim Bob and Bill came closer, he glanced up, smiled thinly, and then pretended to ignore them as he flipped off the pump, returned the nozzle to its cradle, and leaned into the driver's side window of the T-Bird. He stood back up and turned.

Jim Bob was grinning a half-toothed grin and opened his mouth to say something. Sam figured that whatever it was, it had taken the idiot the entire walk from the office to come up with it and he was eager as hell to spit it out. It never happened. Before Jim Bob could say a word, there was a crash from the direction of the office. They all turned. Earl flew back out of the door, arms pinwheeling crazily as he fought for balance. There was a loud CRACK! And he stopped flailing, just for a second. Then he dropped to the ground like a rag doll and Delilah stepped into sight, the .45 in her hand.

Sam took advantage of the moment. He worked the action on the sawed off shotgun he'd retrieved from beneath the seat and laid it across the top of the T-Bird, aimed straight at Jim Bob's shocked face.

"Well hell," he said. "Looks like you boys and your friend over there had a party planned and you weren't even going to invite me. Now what am I going to do with you?"

Bill and Jim Bob's jaws dropped as the shotgun came in line first with one of them, and then the other, sort of hovering in between. Bill gurgled something that might have been "Fuck," but Sam couldn't be sure. Delilah had returned to the office. A moment later, she slammed out the door. In one hand she held a large, heavy cooler by its handle. Her other hand held the .45, and it was leveled at Jim Bob's back.

"You okay, Delilah?" Sam called.

"Bastard came up behind me and ran his hand between my legs, so no, not okay. Not by a long shot. At least the beer is cold."

"That's swell, but we've got us a couple of problems here." He squinted, read the name tags on his two captive's shirts. "Bill and–Jim Bob, is it?"

Delilah sat the cooler down by the front fender of the T-Bird.

"We won't give you no trouble," Bill sputtered. "Ol' Earl weren't right in the head, but–"

Delilah stepped forward and pressed the barrel of the .45 smack in the center of Bill's forehead.

"Shut up. Not another word. I have been speaking English all my life and I am tired of hearing it butchered. You hear me you Beverly Hillbillies reject?"

She turned to Sam and cocked an eyebrow. "You out of ammo, cowboy?"

Sam glanced down at the shotgun, then back up to meet her gaze.

"Nope," he said.

"Then we don't have a problem."

"Well, yeah," Sam said, "But…"

Delilah sighed. She pulled the trigger. The .45 slug tore through Bill's brain and blew the back of his head off, spattering the asphalt with blood and gristle. Bill slumped. Jim Bob, figuring it was his only option, turned and started to run. Sam glanced at Delilah, then at Bill's twitching body flopping on the parking lot and shrugged. He turned and fired. Jim Bob went into a face-first slide, and then lay very, very still.

"This is getting to be a habit," Sam said. "Not sure it's leadin' anywhere good."

Delilah turned and cupped her hand over her eyes to block the sun. She stared down the road back toward the highway.

"It's leading that-a-way. I'm sorry, but those two were either going to kill you or chase you off, and ol' Earl was going to rape me–maybe worse. I don't really see that there were any other options available. It's about time someone started cleaning this planet up, even if it has to be us."

"Yeah, that sounds about right," Sam said. "Still…"

"Drive, cowboy," Delilah said. "California would have been fun, but I hear Mexico is nice this time of year."

They slid the cooler into the back seat, climbed into the T-Bird, and Sam rolled in a slow circle. He nosed back onto the feeder road and roared off toward 281. Neither of them looked back.

SEVEN

The desert spread out around the big truck for miles in every direction without giving up any sign of civilization. They'd left the dirt road behind and pulled off onto the sandy ground carefully, nosing between rocky outcroppings and continuing into the bleak wasteland until they were sure they couldn't be seen from any direction.

Mule, Kurt, and Verdino stood beside the trailer. Terence and Helen had remained in the cab, where they were sharing a quiet moment and some coffee. They were along for transport only. Now and then they kicked in when circumstances called for it, but mostly they drove and left the rest of the 'mission' to the professor and his boys.

About ten feet away from the side of the truck, a large hole had been dug in the rocky soil. Kurt and Mule both wore heavy gloves. Mule was spinning the threaded end of a large hose to a valve on the side of the truck. At the other end of that hose, Kurt held the nozzle, and when he heard the solid Clunk! of the fitting sealing, he crossed to the hole, dragging the heavy hose behind him. He squatted by the hole and called back to Mule.

"Okay, let 'er rip!"

Mule turned a valve on the truck 's side, and the hose stiff-ened, slid sideways just a bit, and then Kurt banged his hand into the valve on the nozzle, sending a steaming spray of gunk into the hole. He turned away quickly.

"Jesus," he said.

Verdino walked over and glanced down into the pit. He didn't react at all to the sudden stench. He examined the waste matter as it spewed from the hose, nodded, and stepped back toward the truck.

Somewhere deep in the trailer, a pump chugged steadily. Kurt held on valiantly to the far end of the hose. Mule watched him, a big grin splitting his face. Now and then he glanced at a set of gauges near the valve. Verdino paced slowly, deep in thought. None of them spoke. Finally, Mule grunted.

"That's it," he said. "Tanks are clean."

"Thank God," Kurt said.

Mule killed the valve, and a moment later, Kurt grabbed the handle on the nozzle and yanked it back shutting off the last trickle of waste.

"That," he said, nodding toward the pit, "is nasty."

"Interesting," Verdino said. "That was a special batch–hasn't been in the tank very long. We could have held the waste until we reached the lab and a proper disposal facility, but under the circumstances…"

"I know," Kurt said. "We can't be hauling something like that around the country. Knowing we had to dump it doesn't stop it from smelling to high Heaven, though."

"No," Verdino said. "I suppose not. Let's get that filled in properly and get the hose stowed. We want to be gone from here and back on the road before too much longer."

Helen stuck her head out the passenger side window of the truck's cab. "We ready to roll?" she said.

"Almost," Mule said. "Give us another fifteen minutes."

"Okay, but hurry. We need to find some food. We're starving up here."

Kurt and Mule rolled the big hose up, being careful not to get any of the goopy waste on their boots. They stowed it all in a compartment beneath the truck. Mule grabbed the shovel they'd used to dig the pit, and Kurt dragged out a spade. The two worked quickly and efficiently, dropping the dirt back over the edge into the pit and covering the waste completely. When it was level, they dragged rocks and scrub across it and scuffed the area up to leave it as natural as possible.

"That's good," Kurt said.

"Right. Let's get the hell out of here. I need to get cleaned up – maybe with some kind of acid. I'm not sure that smell is ever coming out."

They stowed their tools and the soiled gloves with the hose, closed and sealed the compartment, and climbed up into the trailer. Verdino was already inside. When the door was closed, he turned and tapped on the hatch separating them from the cab. It opened and Helen leaned back.

"Ready," Verdino said. "Food and fuel."

"Roger," Helen said. She closed the door. Verdino, Kurt, and Mule took their seats along the side of the trailer. The big truck lurched slightly, bounced, and then slowly made its way across the rough terrain toward the feeder road, and the highway beyond.

EIGHT

The T-bird was parked outside room nine of one of the rattiest motels off Highway 281. The place was laid out in a rough horseshoe shape. At one end the dim lights of the office proclaimed VACANCY in red neon. There were fifteen rooms, two beside the office, three at the far end, and ten in a line down the center. Each had its own parking place. Only one other slot was filled. A beat-up pickup truck was parked outside number three.

The sun had risen, and the day begun, but you couldn't tell it from the place's bleak exterior. It looked more like a scene from an old western movie than a real place. The red neon sign had faded to a pink blur.

In room nine, Sam and Delilah lay back on the bed and watched a small flat screen TV. On the floor beside the bed, the cooler rested, considerably lighter than when they'd first loaded it into the T-Bird.

The room wasn't much. There was the single bed in the center beneath a cheap print of the desert, complete with Saguaro cactus and rolling tumbleweeds. There were worn night stands on either side. One held a cheap digital clock radio. Both had lamps. There was a table beneath the window at the front of the room with two chairs. The bathroom sported a shower and a toilet that ran constantly.

Sam popped the top on a beer and saluted Delilah with it.

"Ol' Earl may have been a bastard," he said, "but at least he had beer."

Delilah snorted and shook her head. "We should have taken our chances and stayed closer to the main road. At least if we'd stopped along there, all we'd have gotten was gas."

Sam grabbed the remote control and started flipping through channels. They'd been watching the end of an old cop movie. It was black and white and grainy, and for some reason the chase scene in progress was just too depressing. He settled on a newscast.

"Maybe they'll have something about the Sunny-Side-Up," he said. "If nothing else, we might find out what they know, whether they're chasing us, and how far behind they are. Hope we have time to finish the beer, at least."

On the TV a slick, dark-suited anchorman with a plastic smile grinned into the camera.

"And now," he said, "for one of the most bizarre stories in recent history. We have Rebecca Wyatt reporting live from the Sunny-Side-Up Coffee Shop. Rebecca?"

The parking lot of the coffee shop filled the screen. It was empty, except for a couple of State Trooper's cruisers and a television news van. In the center of the lot, with the coffee shop perfectly centered in the background, a blonde reporter who looked like a clone of every Barbie doll ever made wrapped into one tight, short-skirted package, frowned thoughtfully back at them. The camera drew in close.

"Here at the Sunny-Side-Up Coffee Shop, something very

strange has happened. Overnight, the owner, customers and staff have simply disappeared. No doors were locked. No sign of breaking and entering, or foul play is in evidence; these people are simply missing. I'm here with State Trooper James Goodman. Officer Goodman, can you shed any light on this?"

Sam turned to Delilah.

"What the hell?"

"Shhh," Delilah said.

On screen, Rebecca held the microphone out to a tall State Trooper sporting a creased uniform and bright, mirrored sunglasses.

"We have very little to go on. At this time, there's no evidence of an actual crime. Local witnesses say the condition of the coffee shop—which is immaculately clean—combined with the fact that the grill was left dirty are an indicator that the owner, Mort Templeton, didn't leave under his own power. An alleged customer, one Stan Langston, is also missing. His scooter was parked out back of the coffee shop, but he hasn't been seen near his apartment for two days."

"So, there's no evidence of foul play?" Rebecca said. Somehow, she managed to make that statement sound less "Scooby Doo" than it was.

"Not at this time," Goodman said. It was impossible to read his expression with the sunglasses on, but his mouth was set in the grim lines so common to cops. "Our investigation is ongoing. We still have a number of missing persons to locate."

Rebecca turned back to the camera and flashed a smile meant to refocus the world on her perfect teeth.

"And there you have it," she said. "A bizarre story unfolding here in the desert. We'll be following this one closely, and you'll get the facts as soon as we have them. Back to you, Wes..."

Sam and Delilah sat in shock, staring at the screen as the

inanely grinning anchorman returned. Sam lifted the remote and turned the set off, then turned to Delilah.

"No sign of foul play?" Delilah said. "What's going on, cowboy?"

"Damned if I know," Sam said. "Still, I'm betting they won't be able to miss our three new friends back at the gas station."

"Well," Delilah said. "I need another beer. This calls for a celebration."

Sam stared at her. "Are you mental?"

Delilah grinned. She took the beer from his hand, drained it, and dropped the can over the side of the bed. Then she slowly slipped across to straddle him and ground her hips against his. She slid up so that their eyes were only inches apart, and then she kissed him, slowly and deeply. Pulling back, she smiled again.

"Probably. Is that a problem?"

Outside the window, there was a sudden flash of lightning. In the distance, thunder rolled and rumbled.

"Perfect," Sam said. He reached over and turned out the light, then drew her down into another kiss. The storm rolled in and over the motel, and the rhythmic pounding of the rain drowned out the world.

NINE

Rain pelted the windshield of the truck, and Terence squinted through the slapping wiper blades at the road ahead. Helen sat beside him, glancing nervously down at the fuel gauge, which was swinging dangerously close to the empty mark. Terence watched her and scowled.

"You got a plan for fueling up?" she said.

"You didn't see the sign? There was a sign for gas a couple of miles back."

"That sign that was hanging by one screw? The rusty one that really just says 'as'? That sign?"

"That's the one."

"You aren't just a little concerned that it might be closed? It's late, and that didn't look like it was pointing to an Exxon with a mini-mart."

"It'll be open. I've been through here before. Boys that run the place are a rough crowd, but they'll have diesel."

"I hope you're right. We aren't going to make it to another exit."

The headlights gleamed off a sign on the right, and Terence

slowed the rig, rolling off the highway. A moment later, the door separating the cab from the trailer opened, and Professor Verdino stuck his head through. He glanced at the rain-streaked windshield, realized he wasn't going to see anything through the rain, and turned to Terence.

"Problem?" he asked.

"Just pulling off to fuel up, Prof," Terence said. "We'll be back on the road before you know it."

Verdino didn't retreat. He stood still, watching as they rolled down the bumpy, secluded road. The lights from the service station came into sight and grew brighter as they approached. Their illumination cut through the rain and brought the world back into focus. Terence turned into the parking lot slowly.

"What the hell is that?" Terence said. He pressed the brake harder than he intended, and the truck slid slightly on the wet pavement as it shuddered to a halt.

"What?" Verdino said.

"There," Terence said. "By the pump." He pointed at the gas pumps. On the ground beside them, two dark lumps lay very still.

"Don't drive over them, whatever they are," Verdino said.

"Wasn't planning on it. You see the door?"

Verdino and Helen followed Terence's gaze toward the station's office. The door hung open. There was only a dim glow from the interior. Though the lights out front indicated that the station was open, the office seemed to be abandoned.

Helen rolled down her window, stuck her head out and used her hand to shield her eyes from the rain. She drew back in and turned.

"Those are bodies," she said.

"Damn it," Terence said. He turned to Verdino. "I hate to say it, Prof, but… here we go again."

The rain hadn't slowed. If anything, it was pouring harder and faster than it had been when they first arrived. Beneath the glaring, rainbow-haloed lights, Kurt and Mule worked steadily. They wore black rain slickers and rubber boots, and they scrubbed with long-handled brushes at the spots where Earl, Bill, and Jim-Bob's bodies had lain only a half an hour before.

Terence was topping off the truck's tanks, watching the meter on the diesel pump spin lazily. It was an old pump, and it was slow. He kept his head down, water running off the bill of his ball cap.

Professor Verdino and Helen stood in the small office, watching the proceedings through the haze.

"It's just like at the coffee shop," Mule said, scrubbing at a particularly stubborn bloodstain. "Except here there's two dead from a handgun, and the other guy blown in half by a shotgun. I'd say it was sawed off from the damage and fired at close range."

"I don't care what kind of gun it was," Kurt said. "I hope whoever did it isn't still around."

"Would you be?"

The stains faded under their relentless attack, but dim outlines remained, no matter how hard they scrubbed, or how much of the chemical cleanser they applied. Terence had finished filling the truck and climbed back into the cab. Helen came running from the office, a newspaper held over her head to block the worst of the rain. A moment later, Verdino followed, closing the door behind him.

"That was open when we got here," Kurt called to him. "You sure you want to close it?"

"There were dead bodies here when we got here. Better not to leave it looking as if something is missing. Better to let it seem abandoned, like the coffee shop." He glanced down at the faded stains. "Those aren't going to fool them for long if they are actually looking for bodies."

"You don't think finding a gas station with the power on, the cash register full, the pumps operating, and nobody home is going to make them suspicious?" Mule asked.

"I'm sure it will, but by that time we'll have a full load and be back at the lab. No one will be the wiser. You two stow that gear. You've gotten it as clean as it's going to get. By the time this rain stops it will look like one more group of oil stains in a very old parking lot."

Kurt and Mule gratefully carried their brushes and the cleaning solvent to the storage beneath the trailer.

"What the hell is going on?" Kurt asked, once they were out of earshot of the others.

"No idea man. Whoever's wiping out the citizens, we're right on their tail; that much is sure. What are the odds we'd find the same run-down gas station they'd hit?"

"They're doing the same thing we are, staying off the main road whenever possible. There were a lot of other stations back a ways, but they were out in the open. Too many people."

"You're probably right. Whatever's going on, I hope we stop somewhere tonight. I've had it with sleeping in the truck, and *you* need a freaking shower."

"Not anymore," Mule said. He pulled back the hood of his slicker and danced a quick jig in the rain."

Kurt turned toward the truck, shook his head, and tried not to laugh. Under his breath he muttered, "Freak."

TEN

Aflashing neon sign glimmered through the rain. The Saguaro Inn Motel came slowly into focus, and Terence eased on the brakes, slowing the big rig for the turn into the parking lot. Helen sat between Terence and Verdino, eyeing the rooms and the dim lights.

"Nice place," she said.

"It's the only place," Terence muttered. "I've driven this route plenty of times. There's nothing else for about thirty miles. If we're stopping, this is it."

"It will be fine," Verdino said. "I'm sure they have showers and beds, and at this point that's what we all need. It's been a rather interesting couple of days."

Terence pulled the truck through the lot and parked it skillfully in the back, lining it up along the edge of the parking lot. The rooms were laid out in a horseshoe shape, and he moved well beyond the last of them, leaving the drive clear for any unlikely traffic.

When they had rolled to a complete stop, Verdino opened the passenger side door and stepped down.

"I'll take care of the rooms. Make sure everything is secured and locked, and have the others get their gear ready. Nothing important stays in the truck, nothing dangerous goes to the rooms. You know the drill."

"You got it," Terence said.

As Verdino closed the door and headed through the drizzling rain toward the motel's office, Terence scanned the parking lot. He caught sight of a black, 1966 T-Bird glimmering in the dim light, parked outside one of the rooms. He stared at it for a moment, frowning.

"What is it?" Helen asked. They'd rolled over a lot of miles of road together, and she sensed his concentration.

"Not sure," Terence said. "It's that car–something about it. I've seen it before, but I just can't place it."

"You can tell you've seen it before in the dark in the middle of a rainstorm?"

"You don't see many like that still on the road," Terence said. "It'll come to me. I guess we'd better climb in back and get the boys moving."

Helen nodded, turned, and climbed through the custom door into the trailer. Terence sat for a moment, staring at the T-bird and trying to remember.

They'd gathered in a single hotel room, none of them quite ready to sleep. Verdino, Terence, Kurt and Mule sat around the room's rickety table eating sandwiches. They had a fairly well-stocked kitchen in the truck, and they'd loaded it up just before hitting the diner. Despite the day's grisly activities, their appetites were solid. Helen lay on the bed, flipping through the few available channels on the TV. She stopped on the news.

"Uh oh," she said. Check this out."

They all turned to see Rebecca Wyatt, reporting on-scene from the Sunny-Side-Up Coffee shop. The reporter stood alone beneath an umbrella in the center of the parking lot. No one else was in sight.

"It seems that there will be no easy resolution to today's mystery. State police have asked for callers with information about the missing proprietor and his staff, but little of interest has surfaced. Mort Templeton and his long-time customer, Stan Langston are missing, as well as one Delilah Martin. No sign of a struggle has been unearthed, and no clues to the whereabouts of these missing persons has been revealed. The investigation is still ongoing..."

Helen muted the TV. Rebecca Wyatt kept on talking, but no one could hear her.

"They're going to be chewing on that one for some time to come," Helen said. "But who is Delilah Martin?"

"I have no idea," Verdino said, "but let's just hope they don't find the gas station too quickly. If we have time to distance ourselves, the odds of things getting complicated will diminish."

Mule and Kurt exchanged a glance, and then they both returned to their sandwiches with a shrug. Suddenly, Terence dropped his onto his plate and smacked his hand down on the table hard, sending plates rattling and sliding in all directions. Kurt and Mule both bobbled their sandwiches. Mule managed to snag his before it hit his lap or the floor, but Kurt held only bread. The meat, mustard and mayonnaise were spread wide across his chair and his lap.

"Dude!" Mule growled, standing with his sandwich gripped tightly "What is wrong with you?"

"Nothing," Terence said, ignoring their anger. "I just figured it out."

"Figured what out?" Kurt sputtered, trying to wipe the sandwich up with the bread and smearing it across his pants. "Damn!"

"That car outside, the old T-bird. I told Helen I'd seen it before, but I couldn't remember where, or when."

"And?" Verdino said. He crossed the room to the small restroom, dampened a handtowel, and brought it back to Kurt, who took it sheepishly.

"It was at the coffee shop. When we pulled in, that car was pulling out. Don't know why it didn't occur to me before–they have to know what happened."

Verdino scratched his chin thoughtfully. "Now that you mention it, I do remember a car taking off. Didn't think anything about it because we didn't know yet."

"Yeah," Terence said. "Exactly. No reason to think about it then, and too busy to remember it when we got inside."

Kurt glanced up from trying to clean off his jeans.

"You're telling me that whoever blew holes in all those people is staying at this same motel?" He turned to Verdino. "The desk clerk when we arrived. He was alive, right?"

Verdino nodded. He stepped around to the window and glanced out to where the T-Bird was clearly visible.

"So," Helen said, "What do we do?"

"I suggest we get some rest. I'll take the room closest to the office, Helen and Terence can stay here. Kurt, you, and Mule take the room in between. Lock your doors, keep the safety chains in place, and stay away from that car. They have no reason to hurt us. They'll probably be gone before we start out."

"You're serious?" Kurt said. "We just stay here and forget about it? We do nothing?"

"What would you have us do? Call the police and say 'the killers you're looking for are staying at the Saguaro Inn Motel. We've been following them and cleaning up their mess, but we'd really appreciate you taking them away. They make us nervous, and we really do need some sleep."

"But…"

"Get some rest. If we tried to leave now, we'd draw their attention. They might figure out what we know and come after us. Better we pretend they aren't here."

"Easy for you to say," Mule growled. He finished the last bit of his sandwich and wiped his mouth with the back of his hand.

Verdino handed him a key and headed for the door. With another shrug, Kurt and Mule rose to follow.

"You sure, Prof?" Terence said.

"I'm sure. It will be fine. Everyone try to rest, and we'll get an early start. The quicker we put all of this behind us, the quicker we'll stop looking over our shoulders."

Verdino, Kurt, and Mule stepped out into the rain and closed the door behind them. Terence walked over, locked the door, and set the safety chain in place. He glanced out through the window. A flash of lightning lit the parking lot and reflected off the smooth, shiny black paint of the T-bird. Terence closed the curtains and killed the lights.

"Goddamn rain," he said.

Helen turned off the TV, and they lay on the stiff, lumpy bed, staring into the shadows until sleep at last drew them into deeper shadows.

ELEVEN

The sun rose, glistening off the remnant of the night's storm and bringing the dingy motel to its full, shabby glory. In the parking lot, only the black T-Bird and Terence's rig remained. The pickup had departed for greener pastures, and there were no late arrivals to the party. As the sunlight filtered its way through the tattered blinds of their room and sliced across Delilah's eyes, she yawned, stretched, and rolled onto her side. Sam lay very still, and she watched him, just for a moment, before reaching out to tease her fingernail down his chest.

"Hey, cowboy, you awake? I think we'd better get rolling."

Sam turned and she saw his eyes were open.

"Been awake," he said. "Go take a look out into that parking lot and see if anything catches your attention."

She met his gaze, held it, and then without a word slid off the side of the bed and padded over to the window. She brushed the blinds aside and stared out through the crack. After a moment, she turned back.

"That what I think it is?" she asked.

"I believe it is," he said. "That's the rig that pulled into the Sunny-Side-Up when we were leaving."

"Christ," she said. "So…what do we do?"

"Damned if I know," Sam said. "Maybe nothing. It could be a coincidence."

"You believe that?"

"Not really," Sam said. He sat up and started to get dressed.

"Maybe we'd better go and make their acquaintance?" Delilah said.

"Maybe," he said. "I think, first, we just wait. We'll feel kind of silly if they just get up, climb in their truck and leave. If they were the kind of trouble we're really worried about, there'd be cops."

He crossed to the window, took another glance out at the truck, and then turned. He watched as Delilah dressed, and when she caught him looking, she smiled.

"What are you looking at, freak?" she laughed. "See something you like."

Sam grinned. Then he frowned.

"What?"

"Just wondering about something," he said.

"Thirty-six D," she said.

"Not that. This. Someone cleaned that coffee shop up so well that the State Troopers couldn't find any trace of "wrongdoing"–I'm thinking, maybe it was the guys in that truck."

"Why in the hell would they do that?"

"A very good question."

"I hate unanswered questions."

Sam stepped away from the window and started gathering up their few belongings. Delilah took the gun, tucked it into the waistband of her pants, and dropped her shirt over it.

"Let's get our stuff into the car," Sam said. "Never hurts to be ready."

"'I guess that old line about being born that way is too lame…'"

"You look like that," Sam said, "you can use any old line you want. And don't forget what's left of the beer."

Sam opened the door, stepped outside, and headed for the T-bird. After grabbing the cooler and giving the room a final once-over, Delilah followed.

. . .

As Sam stepped up to the T-Bird, Terence exited his own room a few doors down. He glanced over, but there was no way to read his expression through the dark sunglasses he wore. He turned and continued toward the truck. Sam stood watching the big man's back as Delilah stepped up beside him and slid the cooler into the back seat.

"We should just get this over with and go on over there," he said.

"Don't hold back on my account, cowboy. What's the worst that could happen?"

He turned and met her gaze evenly. "Never ask that. Never."

Sam turned and started walking slowly across the parking lot toward Terence and the truck. Delilah followed. She turned to glance at the other rooms as they passed, and the curtain fell back across the window of Kurt and Mule's window. Delilah shook her head and laughed.

"Well," she said, "I guess any doubt about whether they know who we are is out the window."

"Guess I'll be glad only one of them had the balls to come outside, then."

Before they could reach the truck, the sound of crunching gravel drew their attention, and they turned. A flashy red

Porsche 911 wheeled into the parking lot, moving faster than was prudent. It rolled past them, and the driver, a blonde in her late twenties, sunglasses perched on her hair and a brilliant white smile flashing like a beacon, waved. She drove to where Terence was inspecting the truck and pulled up beside it.

"What the hell?" Delilah said.

"Nice car," Sam added.

Terence turned. He saw the girl and the Porsche, and then, glancing past her, saw Sam and Delilah.

"Amanda," he said. "What the hell are you doing all the way out here?"

"Hello Terence. Daddy had something he needed delivered to Gregory. I volunteered to bring it for him. You know how Daddy likes to keep track of his investments, and you know how *I* like to keep track of Gregory." She hesitated, turned, and smiled at Sam. "Introduce me to your friends?"

Terence turned to face Sam.

"I'd be happy to," he said, "Just as soon as they introduce themselves to me."

"Terence, huh?" Sam said. "They grow 'em big wherever you come from."

Terence flexed his arm, and Sam caught the motion. The hand was concealed behind Terence's leg. Delilah caught it too and smiled. She rested her hand on her hip, only inches from the butt of the .45.

"Now, now, relax. There's no need for any of that, I'm sure."

Verdino's voice cut through the heaviness of the moment cleanly, and they all turned to stare openly as he calmly crossed the parking lot toward them.

"Amanda," he said. "So good to see you."

Sam turned to Delilah.

"I think this is about to get interesting," he said.

"Trust me, cowboy," she said, "it's already interesting."

"I believe that there is a diner right across the street," Verdino continued. "I think we should all head over there and discuss this over some coffee, eggs and bacon. You do like diners, don't you?"

Delilah laughed.

"He's got us there, cowboy."

Kurt and Mule followed at what they thought might be a safe distance behind Verdino.

Sam shrugged. "Why not?" he said. "Whatever happens next is bound to be better with bacon."

They turned and headed across the parking lot in a tight group. The tension wasn't gone, but the scents of brewing coffee and frying bacon had already begun to work their magic.

TWELVE

*T*he last remnant of the storm had dried away, and the sun beat down on the empty lot of the old service station. The office door was closed. The lights still glowed far overhead, but it was nearly impossible to tell in the brighter light of the sun. The silence was broken by the steady rumble of a big V-Twin engine, and a few moments later, the bike came into sight around the curve.

Jason Kane had been on the road for a long time. The fat bob tanks on his ride could take him close to two hundred miles, but he was pushing it, and he knew he'd have to fill up if he intended to make it the rest of the way to Tucson. It was what he got for taking the smaller roads instead of just hitting Highway 10 and gunning it. He'd just begun to wonder if he'd made a mistake taking the exit by the battered sign when the service station shimmered into view.

His bike was loaded down, full saddlebags and his sea bag, the last remnant of twenty years in the US Navy, strapped to the sissy-bar in back. Address tags and patches lined the surface of the bag, tracing the years and miles behind him.

He pulled into the lot and rolled up to the pumps, scanning the lot for an attendant. He saw that the office was closed, but he also saw that there was a table set up outside. There were beer cans on that table, and something else. He killed his engine and dropped the kickstand.

He pocketed his keys and crossed the lot toward the card table. As he approached, he saw that there were three hands laid face down, and a deck of cards. It was rain soaked. Beer cans littered the table and the ground. There was a soggy pack of smokes beside the chair closest to the office.

Jason glanced around. There was nothing to hear but the wind.

"Anyone here?" he called out.

There was no answer. He walked slowly around the back of the building. The hairs on his arms prickled, but there was no sign of any reason he should be worried. He thought about the winding, empty road. He thought about the half-broken sign, dangling from a single screw that had directed him to this place. He thought about the plots of nearly a hundred bad 'B' grade horror flicks that started just like the scene he was standing very alone in.

"Jesus," he said.

He hurried his steps and circled the station, but there was nothing to see.

He stared at the closed office door. He turned and glanced at his bike. He could just fill it, tuck the money for the gas under the office door, and be on his way. Except, he knew he couldn't. Something was wrong, and he didn't want to take off leaving his prints on some dollar bills that led trouble straight to his doorstep.

"Christ," he said softly. "Why is it always me?"

He pulled his cell phone from the leather sheath that held it clipped to his belt and with a heavy sigh, he dialed 911.

* * *

The parking lot was covered in crisscrossing lines of yellow crime-scene tape. There were chalk outlines on the pavement where Jim Bob, Earl, and Bill had died. The area where Verdino's truck had parked was roped off as well. Officer Goodman's cruiser was parked in one of the clean areas, as was a large white panel truck bearing the logo of the Crime Scene Investigation Unit. There was also a Sherriff's car, as well as Jason's bike.

The Sheriff, who'd just arrived, stood with Goodman, being brought up to speed on the scene. Jason was giving his statement for the third time to a second trooper, George Alberts, who stood with him near his bike.

Goodman glanced up as a young lab technician, Clarence Krizzle, affectionately known as "Skeeter," approached

"What you got Skeeter?" Goodman asked.

"Skeeter?" the sheriff asked.

"Skeeter Krizzle," Goodman said, "meet Sheriff Cicero Brogan. Brogan, Skeeter is one of the sharpest techs I've ever worked with."

"I'm not sure," Skeeter said. "There is definitely blood, but it's been scrubbed. I'd say they used some kind of industrial cleaner. No way to get any sort of match, or DNA off of it."

"Skeeter?" Brogan repeated.

Krizzle turned to the sheriff and grinned. "I take my job very seriously," he said. "A couple of years back we had a homicide. There was nothing to go on, except that there were a number of mosquitos present that we determined might have fed on the killer. I was able to extract enough blood from their bodies to get a DNA match. Clarence Krizzle, at your service." He extended his hand.

Brogan shook it. "Skeeter will do. What kind of industrial cleaner?"

"Not sure yet. I'll have to get all the samples back to the lab for analysis, but it's strong stuff. Nothing that they'd have on hand at a buzzard-bait gas station in the middle of the desert."

"What are you saying, Skeeter?" Goodman asked. "We're looking for killers who brought their own cleaning materials with them?"

"Somebody did," Skeeter replied. "I may know more on that when I get those tire marks cast. That should take about ten minutes or so. After that, we have about all we're going to get here."

Brogan glanced over to where Jason stood beside the other trooper.

"Reckon we'd better let that boy get on his way soon too," he said. "He doesn't look like much, but I saw a couple of the unit tags on that sea bag–he's a vet–and damned if he wasn't going to leave money for the gas."

"I let him fill up," Goodman said. He wasn't going to make it to anywhere from here on empty. In any case, doesn't look like he's carrying any cans of cleaning fluid on that bike. I figure as soon as he finishes that statement, we'll cut him loose."

"Sounds about right," Brogan said. "You'll send me copies of the reports?"

"Of course," Goodman said. "The minute I have anything back from the lab."

The two men shook hands, and Brogan walked back to his cruiser. A moment later he pulled slowly out, winding around the crime scene and back onto the worn feeder road. Goodman watched him leave, then turned and walked over to Officer Alberts and Jason.

"You about done over here?" he asked.

"Yes, sir," Alberts replied. He flipped his notebook closed. "He doesn't know anything."

"That makes a whole bunch of us. You're free to go son. We have your contact information in case we need you?"

"Yes sir," Jason said. "I've given the officer my cell phone and the number and address of the friend I'm going to visit in Tucson."

They all watched as Skeeter carried several cases of materials, tools, and samples back toward his van. Goodman shook his head.

"You have a good ride, son. Next time, I believe I'd get my gas on the main drag."

"You got that right," Jason said.

He stretched and then slid his leg over the bike and kicked it to life. The big motor caught first try and thrummed with power. Goodman nodded again, this time in appreciation.

"It's a sweet machine," he said.

"I take good care of her," Jason said. "Out here, she's all I've got."

A moment later the bike turned out in the same slow curve that Sheriff Brogan had taken. Goodman returned to his cruiser. Ten minutes later, the station was as abandoned as they'd found it, only the yellow crime-scene tape flapping in the wind.

THIRTEEN

Directly across the road from the Motel was the Blue Eagle Diner. The place was low-slung and nondescript. It looked like a thousand other roadside pit stops across the nation. The parking lot was stained with gas, oil, and diesel. Even at this early hour, there were several cars in the lot, and the orange neon sign in the window blinked OPEN to the world.

On the roof, smoke curled lazily from a very old stove-pipe vent. Daily specials stretching back weeks, maybe years, faded slowly on the dusty windows. A sand-filled ashtray stood just outside the door.

The interior was dimly lit and smoky. The stale scent of old cigarettes, cigars, and pipes blended with the more savory aromas of frying bacon and toasting bread. An old man with wavy gray hair worked the grill, lining up link sausages like soldiers and expertly cracking eggs.

The tension between Sam, Delilah, and Verdino's crew was still present, but it had been mellowed by several cups of coffee, plates of pancakes, eggs, and mountains of hash browns. Two men sat at the main counter, eating, and drinking their coffee in silence. The sun trickled in through the patterns of dust on the windows and illumined the dust motes floating in the air.

Verdino pushed his plate away, poured more coffee from the carafe on the table and leaned forward.

"So," he said. "Here's how I see it. What we have here is a unique opportunity."

"Opportunity for what?" Sam asked. "Delilah and I had a problem. You solved it–or at least complicated it–and now it's everyone's problem. Unless I'm confused, or you are, there's not much opportunity in that."

Verdino waved his hand. "Where you see a problem, I see solutions, young man. I can assure you, there is very little left of your problem, and most of what was left we purged through a rubber hose a hundred miles or so back."

"Jesus," Delilah said.

"He hasn't much to do with it, I'm afraid. The man you knew as Mort, his friend Stan, and the three Neanderthals from that gas station have met a timely end. You may be pleased to know that they've been reduced to one part high-grade diesel, and one part sludge. The sludge received a proper, if poorly attended, burial."

"You…you turned them into … gas?" Sam said.

"To put it very simply, yes," Verdino said. "That is exactly what we did. Green, energy-efficient bio-fuel."

"We don't call it gas," Kurt cut in, sipping his coffee. "We call it 'Killer Green.'"

Delilah snorted. "You mean," she said, "Killer Green is… people!?"

Kurt and Mule grinned. Terence and Sam shook their heads. Verdino seemed not to get the reference at all, and Amanda was already smiling.

"I still don't see any opportunity in this, unless you mean the opportunity to get away with murder," Sam said. "I can see how the last day or so might give the impression that killing is what we do, but honestly, it's just circumstances."

"I understand that." Verdino said. "Believe me; if I thought you were cold-blooded killers, I wouldn't be sitting down to breakfast with you. But there's more. We're doing our part to save the planet, and we have a schedule to keep. Amanda's father, our benefactor, will not wait forever. I'm afraid that the small amount of material we've managed to gather and process isn't going to be enough to convince him to continue funding."

"So?" Sam said.

"What I'm suggesting is a partnership."

"What?" Delilah said, leaning forward.

"Relax," Verdino said, still smiling. "I'm not suggesting we go on a killing spree. A situation has come to my attention that is worthy of our attention."

"Hold on there Mr. Bean," Delilah said. "When, exactly, did it become 'our' anything? I don't remember signing on to join the big green machine. In fact, when I crossed the parking lot this morning, I was pretty sure I was going to have to give you more raw material than you could use, being too dead to process it."

"Correct me if I'm wrong, but the two of you don't seem to have any real plans for the near future. Where were you headed, Mexico? If so, the proposition I was about to make involves a flood zone near the Gulf. As the saying goes; since you're going our way?"

"So we're clear," Sam said. "What you're suggesting is that we travel together down to some flood zone near Mexico so we can help you gather up dead bodies and do our part for the environment? Sort of public service without the getting arrested and executed part?"

"Something like that," Verdino said. "Yes."

Sam looked at Delilah, and the two of them burst out laughing. Everyone in the diner turned to watch, but they made no effort to quiet their outburst.

"What in the hell is so damn funny?" Terence asked.

Delilah turned to him. "Come on Snowman," she said. "We shot five people and left them to die, and instead of going to jail, we get a job offer from a truckload of eco-geeks and a shot at the Mexican vacation of our dreams. You don't find that funny?"

"Snowman?" Amanda said. She frowned, puzzled.

"I'm Bandit," Sam explained.

Amanda looked at Delilah, then Terence, and then at Verdino. "Whatever," she said. "By the way, Gregory dear, I'm coming with."

At this they *all* burst into laughter, except Amanda.

"So," Verdino said steepling his finger in front of him, putting his elbows on the table and leaning forward. "Shall I take that as a yes?"

FOURTEEN

Goodman stood in the doorway of the crime lab and watched Skeeter work. The kid was a genius, he knew, but a strange one. He had his own methods, and he watched way too many versions of CSI on TV. The lab was equipped with all the standard equipment, and then some. At least once a week a requisition crossed Goodman's desk for some new piece of test equipment, or set of chemicals, or an obscure reference manual.

He'd have cut it off long ago, but Skeeter wasn't just obsessed; he was good. He found things that other technicians would have claimed weren't there, and he'd proven adept at supporting his findings in court when the need arose. He should have been working for the FBI or some other government agency, but he preferred the anonymity of the desert and the Texas State Police. As far as Goodman was concerned, that was a big notch in the win column.

On the bench was a cast of a tire track. Beside it lay several computer printouts, some photographs, and a newly opened package. Skeeter was ignoring all of this and concentrating on a short row of test tubes in a rack. He was carefully dipping small strips of litmus paper into each of them, then recording notes on a clipboard before moving to the next.

"What you got, Skeeter?" Goodman said at last.

The young man turned, frowned, and then returned to his work as he talked.

"A whole lot of not so much. I know that the truck is probably a recent COLUMBIA, made by FREIGHTLINER–it's the Cadillac of big rigs–they call it the "condo". It's carrying a big trailer with a slightly uneven load. Not standard."

"What about the chemicals?"

"Kind of weird. Nothing you'd expect to see anywhere outside a laboratory environment. That's serious industrial stuff, meant to cleanse things that normally wouldn't even exist out in the world. Expensive too. I've done a preliminary search. It's at least a hundred miles to the nearest place that sells that kind of chemical, and another fifty to the nearest facility that might need it."

"Still, if' it's not common, we might be able to trace it by the sale," Goodman commented.

"The problem is, if they bought it through any sort of legitimate laboratory, it's going to be rough to trace. Only real chance is if there's an odd buy out there that stands out."

"Figures," Goodman said. "Got anything else?"

"The blood wasn't much use either. The chemicals corrupted any DNA we might have gotten. I was able to match blood types to two of the guys who worked at the gas station from previous arrest and medical records, but a blood type match isn't much to go on. There was no third employee, so I have no idea who that was. Without bodies …"

"Yeah, I know," Goodman said. He turned toward the door, then glanced back over his shoulder.

"You get anything else–anything at all–you let me know."

"You got it Chief," Skeeter grinned.

Goodman sighed and left the lab.

*   *   *

Back in his office, Goodman sipped a fresh cup of coffee and stared at the phone. After a minute, he put the cup down and reached for the receiver. He dialed, leaned back, put a foot up on his desk, and waited.

The phone rang once, twice, and then Brogan's brusque voice came on the line.

"Sheriff's office, Brogan," he said.

"It's Goodman," he said.

"Hey," Brogan said. "You got something?"

"Not much. Skeeter says it's a Freightliner Columbia model truck. Also says those chemicals had to have come from a laboratory of some kind, or to have been ordered from a laboratory supply house. I'm thinking this truck might stick out a bit."

"When you say something like 'not much,' you don't kid around, do you? Okay. I'll have my guys out looking for any sort of oddball truck, or any rig that looks out of place. You think they're still heading south?"

"That's what I'd do, if I was them," Goodman said.

"Yeah, that's what I thought too. You know, there's already some trouble out that way. The flood? Bad stuff."

"Yeah. Still, if you know any of the boys in your office out that way...might be a good idea to give them a call. I'll be doing the same."

"I'll do that. They probably have their hands full, though," Brogan said. "I've got some time coming...might be up for a few days down by the gulf myself. Good for my breathing, you know? A little humidity... a can of Tecaté or two."

"You decide to do that," Goodman said, "you let me know. It's been a while since I was down that way. I've got some friends I could look up."

"Count on it, Officer Goodman," Brogan chuckled. "You just count on it."

Brogan hung up then, and, after staring at the receiver thoughtfully for a moment, Goodman did the same. He thought about the road stretching off toward Mexico and sighed. It was going to be a long, dreary day.

FIFTEEN

The sun had tucked itself away beyond the horizon, and long shadows stretched across the road. Terence drove steadily, following the wavering taillights of Amanda's Porsche. Behind the rig, Sam and Delilah followed in the T-Bird. They'd put a lot of miles behind them, but no one had complained. The Porsche swerved one way, then the other, and then righted itself.

"What the hell?" Terence said.

Then the Porsche sped up, and he pressed the gas, giving chase. On the horizon, the lights of a town glowed dimly, and ahead, on the right, he could just make out the neon outline of a Saguaro cactus.

"Stop it, Gregory!" Amanda said. She slapped his hand where he was running it up her thigh. "Do you want me to wreck Daddy's car?"

"I want something," Gregory said, leering at her and waggling his eyebrows. He glanced ahead, saw the glowing neon of the cactus sign, and lifted his hand from her leg to point. "Let's pull in there. I think it's about time we all got something to eat, and it looks like there's a motel just up the road. We're not going to

make it to the Gulf tonight, so there's no sense in pushing anyone beyond their limits."

"Nice place," Amanda said, eyeing the 30 foot cactus.

She pulled into the parking lot, turning in past a sign that
read "Peyote Slim's Bar & Grill." There were beer and whiskey advertisements all over the windows, and the parking lot
was more than half full. Most of the other vehicles were pickup
trucks, though a couple more big rigs were parked around back.

Amanda slowed to a crawl and turned to Verdino.

"You sure, Gregory? I mean, look at this place. I'm afraid
we're going to stand out a bit, don't you think?"

"We aren't going in looking for trouble," he said. "All we want
is some food. And it's not like we'll be alone. It will be fine."

"Right." Amanda didn't sound convinced, but she wound
through the parking lot toward the back and parked in the last
place before the pick-ups gave way to the trailers.

Terence pulled in and parked as close as he could. Sam
wheeled the T-bird in beside the Porsche, and he and Delilah
climbed out. They were standing, staring at Peyote Slim's when
Terence, Helen, Kurt, and Mule joined them.

"You sure about this?" Terence asked.

"You hungry?" Verdino asked.

"Well, yeah, but…"

"To hell with it," Sam said. "I say we go in, and we eat. What's
the worst that could happen?"

They all turned and stared at him.

"You told me never to ask that, cowboy," Delilah said with
a grin. "If I didn't know better, I'd think you were looking for
trouble."

"Yeah, okay. Every time I ask that, I get an answer. I'm still
fucking hungry. I could go for a burger about now."

"And maybe a beer," Kurt said.

They crossed the parking lot in a tight group. The tinny twang of country music leaked out through the windows. Terence stepped ahead and opened the door, holding it for the rest as they stepped inside.

"Hope we aren't gonna regret this," he said. He followed them in, and the door closed behind them with a Thunk!

The music was loud, but there was laughter, the clack of pool balls from a back room, and a general roar of conversation competing for attention. As they made their way across the floor toward the dining tables, all but the music fell silent. Every head in the place turned to watch them, and the only person still moving was the bartender, a thin man with greasy hair. On the counter in front of him was a large coffee cup in the shape of a naked breast. The sign taped to it said "Tits" but the t was marked through with a diagonal line, and changed to a 'P'.

"Oh boy," Sam said. "This is gonna be fun."

They found a large empty table in the back and seated themselves. Slowly, as the newcomers did nothing of particular interest, the noise returned, until a few moments later it had reached full volume again, and they were all but forgotten.

A waitress grabbed her tray from the bar and headed toward them. She was in her early forties, dirty blonde hair and eyes either too heavily made up, or just tired beyond belief. Her nametag read 'Gladys.'

"How can I help you folks?" she asked as she drew near.

"Food!" Verdino said cheerfully.

She nodded toward the wall to her left. "Everything we have is on that board."

The board had several beer specials. There were sandwiches and burger platters lined up by price. Everything came with fries.

"Maybe we'd better start with some drinks," Sam said. "I could use a beer."

Kurt, Mule, Delilah, Terence, and Helen ordered the same. The waitress made some quick notes on her pad, then turned to Amanda.

"How about you dear?"

"I think I'd like some red wine," she said. She smiled brightly. "Do you have any cabernet?"

The waitress stared at her like she was waiting for a punch line. When it didn't come, she closed her pad, put a hand on her hip, and frowned.

"Honey, we got Boone's farm, and somewhere in the back there's a half-empty bottle of Night Train. Other than that, you got beer, water or …beer."

Amanda bit her lip, and then smiled. "I think I'll try the Night Train," she said. "At least it sounds European…"

They all turned to stare at her. The waitress sighed. She turned to Verdino.

"You?"

"Beer," he said. "Definitely beer."

Gladys turned way, shaking her head, and headed off to the bar for the drinks. Everyone at the table made an effort not to meet Amanda's eyes. After a couple of seconds, she caught on.

"What?" she said.

They studied the chalked menu and fought back their laughter. For the moment, no one in the place was paying them the least bit of attention, and they figured it was best to keep it that way.

...

Sheriff Wayne Rainey pulled slowly into the parking lot of Peyote Slim's, his mind already on the rare burger and salty fries he intended to order when he got inside. He scanned the trucks and beat-up cars as he passed. There'd been some trouble at Slim's over the years, and he knew a lot of those behind it. If they were inside, he wanted to know before he hit the door.

When he saw the Porsche, he did a double take, slowed, and stared. He hadn't seen a car like that at Peyote Slim's in all the years he'd been patrolling the area. He also didn't recognize the shiny black T-Bird beside it. Strangers might mean trouble. He drove past the T-Bird and came to a full stop.

Ahead on the right, tucked in between an old Mack and a Winnebago was a shiny 18-wheel truck that looked out of place in the dusty parking lot. There were plenty of rigs lined up beside and beyond it, but this one didn't look right. It was too new, and too clean. And unless his eyes were deceiving him in the low light…the damn thing was Green.

Rainey reached for the mic on his radio and keyed it quickly.

"Cactus Base? This is Cactus Rover One, over?"

"Cactus Rover One, this is Cactus Base. Five by five, over."

"I think I might have a visual on that truck you called in. The Freightliner? Anyone say what color it was?"

"Negative on the color, Cactus Rover One. What's your twenty, over?"

"I'll get back to you," Rainey said. "I need to check something…Cactus Rover One, out."

He placed the microphone back on its holder and stared up at the truck. He'd made rash calls before, and he wasn't about to make another one if he could help it. He leaned back and watched the truck.

"Well, Wayne," he said. "This could be it. Could be the big one. Then again…it could be one big assed truck full of Idaho potatoes. Better to know what's what before you call it in and make a fool of yourself."

He eased off the brake, pulled his cruiser around the back of the building and around to the other side. There was an empty space that gave him a good angle across the back of the lot straight at the big truck, and he took it. He checked his weapons, and then leaned back to watch, and to wait. He wished the smoke from the grill wasn't washing out over the front of his cruiser; he'd really wanted that burger.

SIXTEEN

The food had arrived, and everyone dug in. They washed it down with cold beer, and even Amanda, who held up like a trooper against the onslaught of fried food and cheap wine, remained silent for a while. The other patrons of Peyote Slim's had lost whatever interest they had in the group and gone back to their own various forms of entertainment. Finally, washing down the last of his burger with a swig of beer, Verdino started to talk.

"The situation down at the Gulf is bad," he said. "They are going to be taking volunteers, and they aren't going to be too particular where they get them. There are probably others headed in now, hoping to offer help. We all have talents to offer, assuming we can be judicious in explaining them, and sometimes all it takes is another able body. By day, we'll work beside all the others. Lives will be saved"

"Then, when night falls, we'll be about our own business."

"You want us to collect dead bodies out of the Gulf of Mexico?" Delilah said. It wasn't really a question, though she at least had the courtesy to phrase it that way. "But, to be clear, it's all in public service, right?"

"You got other plans?" Mule asked. He grinned, and Delilah laughed.

"Got me there. This gig pay?"

Mule glanced at Kurt, then grinned again. "Depends on what you consider pay."

"Everyone who participates will be compensated," Verdino said.

There was an old television hanging over the corner of the bar. It was directly across from where Sam sat, and he happened to glance up at the screen."

"Hold it," he said.

They all turned to follow his gaze. The screen was too small to see clearly, and the club far too noisy. Sam rose and walked over to the bar. He leaned on the counter, not paying attention to anything but the newscast. His arm bumped the drink of a tall, rangy man in a cowboy hat, but Sam didn't even glance over.

On the screen, Rebecca Wyatt stared back at him with her patented, plastic concern turned on full force.

"The scene here at the Desert Moon Gas Station is grim. Owner and manager Earl West is missing, as are a co-worker and one other yet unidentified companion. It has not been confirmed whether this disappearance is related to an earlier incident at the Sunny-Side-Up Diner less than twenty-four hours ago, but Sheriff Cicero Brogan has told us he has not ruled out this possibility. I quote: 'there is evidence here of foul play.' We will be releasing a description of a particular vehicle later today, in cooperation with State Police..."

"Hey," the cowboy beside Sam said.

Sam ignored him and kept his attention on the screen. Then the cowboy grabbed him by the arm and shoved. Hard.

"I said *HEY!* Asshole. You got somethin' in your ears, or you just looking for trouble?"

Sam spun quickly. "What the hell did you do that for?"

"You spilled my drink," the cowboy nodded at the bar.

Sam glanced down and saw a tiny splash of bourbon beside the tumbler on the bar. He glanced back up, and he didn't smile.

"Maybe you want to reconsider," he said.

"*You* need to buy me a new drink," the cowboy said.

Across the bar, two truckers rose and walked slowly toward the bar. "Everything okay, Bob?" one of them asked.

"Everything's fine, Zeke," Bob said. "This boy is just gonna buy me another drink."

The third man stepped forward and looked Sam up and down.

"Maybe you should buy us all a drink, while you're at it. Buncha freaks come in here like you own the place."

The others had risen as soon as Sam was shoved. Verdino, hoping to defuse the impending powder keg of beer and machismo, stepped up beside Sam.

"Gentlemen," he said. "I'm sure we can find some way past this…"

"Like hell," Cowboy Bob said. He cocked back and swung at Sam, who dodged easily. Bob grunted and drew back his fist again, but before he could launch the blow, there was a loud CLICK right near his face.

"I believe," Delilah said calmly, "he said you might want to reconsider."

"Jesus!" Zeke said, backing away. Bob turned and found himself staring down the barrel of the .45. Delilah's hand was steady, and her gaze was cold, though her lip was curled in a smile.

"Hey!" the bartender called from behind bar. "Not in here. Hell no! You all take this outside."

"Shut up Clem," the second trucker said. "There ain't a damn thing you can do about this." He turned to Delilah. "You want to put that thing down, lady, before someone gets hurt."

"You first," she said.

"Don't…" Sam said.

Delilah dropped the barrel of the gun and fired. Wood chips flew between the boots of the two truckers, who scrambled backward, falling ass over elbows. Bob saw his moment and lunged. It was a mistake. Sam caught him full in the face with his beer. The mug shattered, Bob screamed, and the room was showered in beer, foam, and broken bits of glass.

Another guy, skinny with stringy hair and a nose like a rat rose slowly behind Sam. He started forward, but Terence stepped in between. He had a long, wicked blade in his hand.

"Sit down friend," he said. "While it's still an option." He turned then and glanced at Sam, then at the floor where beer had puddled and was spreading out across the stained hardwood. "I think your beer went flat," he said.

Delilah rolled her eyes.

The skinny guy held his ground, but he didn't come any closer. They all grouped together, Amanda in the middle, Delilah covering the bar, and Terence turned to the rear, watching for any sudden moves. Verdino tossed a pair of twenties onto the bar.

"That should cover it," he said.

They moved toward the door, and no one tried to stop them. As they passed the bar, Kurt reached out and grabbed handful of peanuts out of one of the bowls. He shoved them in his mouth, and Mule whacked him on the back.

"Dude," Mule said, "are you fucking serious?"

"What?" Kurt said. "I didn't get to finish my burger. I'm *hungry.*"

"Slide on out," Delilah said. She held the gun steadily, swinging her arm slowly from side to side to cover the entire bar.

Terence followed Kurt and Mule out, and that left just Delilah, alone in the doorway. Cowboy Bob took a step toward her, and she smiled again. This time she meant it.

"Please?" she said.

Bob took another step and Delilah, pulling her finger back, without actually touching the trigger, shook the .45 at him and said "BANG!"

Cowboy Bob dove for cover, and Delilah backed out, letting the door slam closed behind her. Then they were in the parking lot, and moving, leaving the bar, Travis Tritt on the Juke Box, and the screaming rednecks behind.

SEVENTEEN

Sheriff Rainey sat, staring at the bar, and wondering if he should just give it up and go in after that burger. Nothing had happened, and though there was some shouting inside, there was always shouting at Peyote Slim's. If you didn't belong with that crowd, or didn't have a reason to be there, it could get downright unfriendly. Whoever had driven up in that Porsche was likely finding that out.

Then the door opened, and people started pouring out. More people than you'd normally see exiting a bar at the same time, and there was something wrong with the way they were walking. They had their backs to the parking lot, and they were moving too slowly. Might not be the payoff he was hoping for but damned if he hadn't found himself enough trouble to make the night interesting.

He counted five men and two women in the group. Then a third woman backed out of the door, and they all started across the parking lot at a trot, heading toward the big truck, the T-bird, and the Porsche. Rainey watched them until they'd crossed enough of the lot that they couldn't easily rush back inside, or run, and then he reached up and gave a quick WHOOP on his siren.

Terence, who was a little ahead of the others glanced over at Rainey and his cruiser, then back at the bar.

"Oh crap," he said.

Rainey climbed quickly out of the cruiser. He had a shotgun in one hand.

"Hold it right there!" he called out.

"He kidding?" Sam asked

"I don't believe he is, cowboy," Delilah said.

Behind them, Cowboy Bob, Zeke, and the whole crew surged out the door of the bar, rolling into the parking lot like a sweaty, low-IQ wave.

"This just keeps getting better," Mule muttered. "What now?"

"Go!" Sam said. "Run, get in your cars, trucks, whatever, and go. I'll meet you down south of here. Fifty miles, then off the highway."

Without another word, he turned and sprinted for the T-Bird. Delilah glanced at Rainey and his shotgun, then she shrugged and followed. Terence and Helen headed for the truck with Kurt and Mule on their heels. Behind them, moving more slowly, Verdino followed. He looked flustered, as if he couldn't believe there was no calm way to talk his way through whatever was about to happen.

Seeing that their quarry was heading for the hills, the mob surged forward out of the door. Amanda turned, grabbed two fistfuls of Verdino's shirt, and shook him hard.

"Let's *go* Gregory! Can't you see that they have *guns?*"

That did it. Verdino spun and sprinted for the Porsche. Amanda followed, making the act of running in high heels look simple. Rainey watched her for a moment, captivated, then shook his head and raised the shotgun. He fired it into the air.

"I said *halt* damn you!" he screamed.

The mob stopped dead in their tracks when the shotgun went off. Rainey paid no attention to them at all. He saw the ones he was after spreading out across the parking lot toward different vehicles. He didn't hesitate. He could jack up the rodeo clowns at Slim's any night of the week. This one was bigger than that.

He saw the guy he figured for the driver cut around the trailer of the big truck, and he took off after him at a run. He slid around the back of the trailer just as the driver was closing the door. Rainey jacked the pump on the shotgun.

"Hold it right there, big boy," he said. "You step on back down out of that truck nice and slow."

Terence pushed the door back open gently. He turned and leaned out of the cab. Slowly, he raised his hands, and he smiled.

"Yes?" he said."

"You just get down here," Rainey said. "I got some questions for …"

At that moment, there was a whistling sound. The tire iron caught him on the side of the head. He dropped the shotgun, wind-milled his arms, and spun, falling backward.

Terence grinned at Helen.

"Took your time," he said.

"Had to get the iron. Now get in there, start this thing up, and drive," she replied, running around the cab to the passenger side.

Mule and Kurt were already in back, locking the door. Even before Helen was fully seated, the big diesel rumbled to life. Terence took off without warming up, praying it wouldn't stall.

The Porsche and the T-Bird shot across the parking lot, splitting the thronging crowd like a herd of cattle. Verdino drove the Porsche, and once he had it in his mind that they needed to escape, he was focused. He hit the highway in a skid, brought the tires straight, and shot into the darkness. Sam was right behind him, the T-bird's V8 roaring with power. A moment later, Terence had the big rig rolling. He took it slower, steered onto the highway even as he picked up speed, and gave a loud shot at the air-horn as they passed the bar.

The mob milled about, some hesitantly heading for their trucks, or cars. Some heading back inside. They saw Rainey lying on the parking lot, and they didn't know if he was dead or alive. They'd all heard the shot.

Then the sheriff, woozy and blurry eyed, sat up slowly. He shook his head–shot his hand out to catch himself as the pain of that nearly put him under again, then rose slowly to his feet. He turned and stared at the road, where the three vehicles had disappeared. He raised his hand and pointed after them.

"I said *halt!* Damn you." More quietly he added, "Why won't you fucking halt?"

Then he collapsed in a heap, and the crowd rushed forward to help him back to his feet. He was barely coherent, but he managed to turn to the two who'd lifted him to his feet.

"They wouldn't halt," he said. "I don't know why…"

EIGHTEEN

Somehow, they made it out and away from Peyote Slim's without being followed. The Sheriff, whoever he'd been, had gone down for the count, and apparently the redneck posse had determined they'd rather have another beer and talk about how they'd kicked some 'weirdo tail' than follow and take a chance on getting shot. It bought them some time.

Verdino drove the Porsche at around seventy. Amanda had kicked back in the passenger side seat, one shoeless well-manicured foot on the dashboard, and the other tucked up beneath her. She was laughing happily. Verdino turned, shook his head at her, and then failed to stop his own grin.

"That was *fun!*" she said.

"It was at that," Verdino said. "Still, I think you'd better see if you can get your father on the phone. That sheriff will get up eventually, and there's not a lot of places to hide a truck this size between here and Mexico."

Amanda dug in her purse for a moment, pulled out a brand-new glittering Android, encased in a pink, glittery shock case.

You could have seen the pink of it for a city block. With practiced ease, she dialed.

"Daddy?" she said. "Yes, of course it's me, who else would it be? Yes…I found them. Listen, Daddy, Gregory needs to talk to you."

She handed over the phone.

Verdino tucked the phone under his chin and cocked his head so he could keep his eye on the road.

"Mr. Stone? Yes sir, I'm taking good care of her sir. One thing. We've had a turn of good luck, but we're also up against a bit of a snag. I wonder if you could do me a favor?"

He paused, then smiled.

"Yes sir. We should have everything we need within the week. That's the good news I mentioned. Unfortunately, we crossed a few more radars than we intended in the process. I need to implement Itinerary B. We'll handle our end in less than an hour. After that I'll coordinate pickup."

He listened again, and then nodded.

"Yes sir…" He grinned "'You can count on it."

He handed the phone back to Amanda and pressed his foot on the gas, shooting up closer to 80mph. On the right, a sign came into view. It read BENSON, 39 Miles. Verdino pointed at it.

"Dear, see if you can get Terence on the phone. Tell him to take the cut-off toward Benson. Tell him that we are going to implement Itinerary B. He'll know what I mean by that."

"You and your code words are so cute," Amanda said. She giggled.

He raised an eyebrow at her, and she punched numbers on the phone 's dial pad.

"Okay, okay," she said. "It's still cute. She held the phone to her ear, listened, spoke for a minute, laughed again, and then hung up.

"He understands, Gregory dear. Let us implement Itinerary B."

Behind them, Sam and the T-Bird whipped out and slid around in between the Porsche and the truck. Verdino smiled.

"I believe I'll see if our friend in the T-Bird is up for a bit of a race," he said.

He floored the Porsche and it shot forward. A moment later the sound was answered by the throaty roar of the big 390 rushing up behind. Amanda laughed again, this time with both feet on the dashboard and her hair flying behind her in the breeze.

Terence grinned as he saw Verdino and Sam tear off into the night.

"Hell of a time for a race," Helen said. "That sheriff back there–he isn't gonna lay down on the asphalt all night. He'll be calling in the cavalry before long, and they're going to be right on our ass."

"The Prof has it covered," Terence said, pressing steadily on the gas and bringing the big rig up to speed. "It's all good."

"Doesn't seem good to me," Helen said. "He's a smart man, Terry, but…this?"

"What," Terence said, winking at her. "Didn't I ever tell you about Itinerary B?"

Helen stared at him.

"No."

"Well," Terence said, turning back to the road. "Probably 'cause it's a secret."

He kept driving, and Helen turned, staring out the window at the passing desert. Terence grinned.

Fifteen minutes later, they saw the exit to Benson, and Terence slowed and made the turn. He continued, more slowly, until they saw a red glow ahead on the road.

"What's that?" Helen asked.

"Flare," Terence said.

He pulled up within about ten feet of the flare and stopped. He left the engine running and climbed down, grabbed the flare, and returned to the truck. He handed it to Helen carefully.

"Hold it out the passenger side window, okay? We'll be going out without the headlights."

Helen took the flare, and Terence slowly turned the truck off the road and headed into the desert, winding slowly around rocky outcroppings and patches of scrub.

"There's another flare out there a way," Helen said.

"There should be two more before we're ready to stop," Terence said. "Take that one into the back, give it to Mule, and tell those boys to get ready for Itinerary B."

Helen stood, holding the flare carefully as the truck bounced over the uneven ground. She opened the door to the trailer, then turned back to Terence.

"That's it? You couldn't come up with anything cooler to call the super-secret escape plan than 'Itinerary B'?"

"I didn't name it," Terence said. He didn't turn to meet her gaze. Shaking her head, Helen stepped into the trailer and closed the door as Terence drove slowly toward the second flare.

...

Kurt, Mule, and Helen had climbed down to stand with the others near the T-Bird and the Porsche. Terence, alone in the cab, positioned the truck carefully. When he was sure it was as level as he could get it, he put the engine in park. Moments later, support legs dropped on the four corners of the trailer, sliding smoothly down until round, flat "feet" hit the rocky ground. Watching a panel on the dash, Terence manipulated the lifts until the trailer was fully level. Another switch opened the rear panel. A set of stairs slid out and down. When he was satisfied, Terence killed the engine and leaned out, giving Verdino a quick thumbs-up.

Verdino returned the gesture, then turned to the others.

"Let's get to work," he said. "We don't have much time."

Kurt and Mule climbed back into the trailer and a moment later they emerged with several small compressors and an armload of power cables. Next, with Sam and Terence's help, they opened panels in the trailer's ceiling and pulled out long, tightly rolled strips of metal. A few moments later, one of the compressors kicked to life.

"I ever tell you what I hate?" Terence said, turning to Kurt.

"Punk Rock?" Kurt guessed.

"Itineraries." Terence said. Then he flipped his safety goggles into place, and they set to work.

All around the truck, rocky crags poked up through dusty soil. Scrub brush and short, twisted trees grew sparsely, creating long, eerie shadows in the bright moonlight. On one side of the trailer, a hill rose slightly higher than the height of the truck. The moonlight cut over the top, washing the trailer in shadows.

A whirring, hydraulic sound broke the silence. A ramp slid out from beneath the rear of the trailer, tilted, and lowered toward the ground. When it was fully extended there was a loud clank that echoed across the barren landscape.

The side door of the trailer opened, and Verdino stepped out. He strode along the side of the trailer, stepped onto the ramp in the rear, and stared into the interior.

Kurt, Mule, and others began carrying more equipment bags out the back, air hoses, and tool bags, and the long, rolled panels they'd removed from the interior ceiling compartment. Next, they stepped up beside the trailer and leaned down. They opened a set of latches and tilted the door of a long, deep compartment out and down. Working quickly and efficiently, they dragged long vinyl rolls out onto the sand.

"Never thought we'd need these," Mule said.

Kurt grinned. "Never say never."

Behind them, another of the compressors kicked into life. A string of lights flickered to life, softly illuminating the small clearing in red. The ruby light dripped off the hill, and the truck, like luminous blood.

NINETEEN

Goodman scanned the shadows to either side of road as he drove south toward Peyote Slim's. The road was empty and dead. He didn't think he'd passed half a dozen vehicles in the last half hour. He reached down, grabbed the microphone on his radio.

"FOURSTAR BASE, this is FOURSTARSIX. I'm currently traveling south on state Highway 281 off Kenefick. That hick town sheriff...was his name Haney? Is he meeting me at the bar?"

There was a moment's silence, and then the radio crackled to life.

"Affirmative FOURSTARSIX–Sheriff Rainey is parked at Peyote Slim's Bar & Grill awaiting arrival."

"Any word on the truck?" he asked. "How about the two cars? You'd think a ride like that Porsche would turn a couple of heads out this way."

"Nothing yet," was the response.

"Roger that," he said. "FOURSTARSIX out."

He saw the bright neon sign from a long way off. He pressed his foot on the gas and sped across that last half mile or so, turning into the parking lot and rolling around the back to where two Sheriff's cruisers were parked, one with the light bar flashing slowly.

As he parked, he saw Brogan, and another man, balding with a short beard, leaning against the driver's side door of one cruiser. Goodman climbed out and walked over, scanning the now nearly empty parking lot.

He stepped up and nodded at Brogan, then turned to the other man.

"You Rainey?" he asked.

The man nodded. He held an ice pack to his temple, and he winced each time it made contact. Most of his weight rested on the cruiser.

"Yeah, that's me," the man said.

"Looks like they caught you a good one. You see who did it?"

"I got a good look at the truck driver," he said. "No idea who hit me. Parking lot was full, and I never heard them coming."

"I got descriptions from the bartender," Brogan said. "There's a group of them. Two women, one dark hair–matches the description of your missing waitress from the Sunny-Side-Up. The others are a mixed lot, some fancy-dressed lady in a Porsche, a bald guy with glasses, two younger guys the bartender says were "nerds," the truck driver, a woman they assumed to be his wife–and the guy in the T-bird."

Rainey glanced up.

"Those descriptions any good?"

"Good enough," Brogan said. "We come up on that group, we'll know 'em. And they can't have gotten too far."

"Witnesses say they took off south," Rainey said. Ain't nothing down that way but state roads, desert, and if you drive long enough, the Gulf."

"We get started," Goodman said, "We might just be able to catch up with them."

"We might at that," Brogan said. Sheriff Rainey, I need you to radio ahead and let the locals down south know we're comin'– and why. Then, if I was you, I'd get that head examined."

"Funny," Rainey said, wincing. "I'll take care of it."

"I knew you would," Brogan said. He turned to Goodman. "You ready for a road trip?"

"Reckon I am," Goodman said. "Let's do it."

The two returned to their cruisers and then, one after the other, rolled out of the parking lot and back onto the road beyond, headed south. Rainey watched them for a moment, holding the ice to his aching head, then turned and climbed into his own cruiser to call in as requested. His head ached like a bitch, and he really needed a beer. The quicker he got this wrapped up, the quicker he'd be home. All thoughts of the big collar had faded into a deep, throbbing ache.

. . .

Out in the desert, work progressed quickly, and efficiently. After popping loose trim around the edges of the trailer, Mule, Kurt, and Terence tugged and freed vinyl panels, rolling them down the sides, then the rear and even the top of the trailer. The sheets came off, rolled up easily, and were tossed aside. Next, the rolls that had been removed from the compartment beneath the truck were smoothed out and snapped in place, using rolls of metal trim from the trailer's ceiling compartment. It transformed the bright green vehicle to a dingy, drab, gun metal gray.

Verdino and Sam, meanwhile, sprayed the cab with solvent, using one of the compressors and a spray gun. The green paint sluiced away as if had been watercolor, revealing dull-brown primer. Then, as the crew finished up with the side, top, and rear panels, Mule connected a portable sandblaster to the compressor, and they took the paint on the wheels down to bare aluminum. The green panels were rolled carefully and stowed beneath the trailer.

With the trailer up on hydraulic stands, the cab rumbled to life, and Terence pulled it forward slowly, until it rested about twenty feet away, idling slowly. Sam broke off from the others and fired up the T-Bird, rolling it slowly up beside Terence. As Kurt and Mule collected and packed the tools and cables back into the trailer, they gathered near the truck's driver's side door. Terence had the window rolled down, and he leaned out so he could see and hear more clearly.

Verdino cupped his hands and hollered over the idling diesel. "Make sure you get it far enough out. We don't want someone finding it too quickly."

"You got it," Terence replied. "I think I can hide it in those rocks about ten miles off. Anyway, the color will throw them off some. I'll turn on the GPS before I leave it–shouldn't be too hard for Mr. Stone to find."

Verdino glanced back at the trailer and smiled thinly.

"Those replaceable panels were a good idea. I'm not sure that *I* would recognize that trailer from a distance."

"Daddy says the new truck and cars will be here in a few hours. He's bringing them up from the south, so they don't draw attention. The roads north are being watched."

"Thank you darling," Verdino said.

"I hate to interrupt the committee meeting," Terence said, "But can we get going? I don't like sitting here like this any longer than we have to."

Verdino nodded. "Good luck," he said.

"Whatever," Terence said. He put the big truck in gear and started it rolling. He picked up speed, cutting a swath of dust as he rumbled across the rough ground toward the rocks he's mentioned. The T-Bird pulled in behind him. Sam waited a moment to give the truck some distance, then shot off after it, spinning tires and throwing gravel.

Verdino stood immobile, watching until both vehicles were small specks on the horizon. Behind him Kurt and Mule applied final touches to the trailer's new face, checking the wheel-wells carefully and tightening the trim over the new panels.

As they worked, Delilah walked slowly around the entire worksite. She ran her hands over the side of the trailer, turning now and again to stare at one or another of her companions. When she'd finished her circuit, she stopped near Verdino, who turned back and smiled.

"What kind of freaks are you people, anyway? You turn bodies into gasoline, you have no problem with avoiding the law; you can call and have a new truck delivered in the middle of the desert? Seriously?"

"Well, this is a special situation. And they're bringing a couple of cars, as well. We don't want to take chances."

"Special?" Delilah said, incredulous. "That's special alright. Short-bus special. Are you kidding me? What happens next?"

"We already discussed that," Verdino replied. "We'll head down south to the Gulf, get taken on as volunteers…"

"Just like nothing happened?" Delilah asked. "Just like half the cops in Texas aren't on the lookout for us now? Just like there isn't a string of dead bodies running all the way from here back to the diner?"

"They are looking for a red Porsche, a black Thunderbird, and a green truck. I don't believe they'll have much luck with any of those. We have a job to do. We are scientists."

"That's what you keep saying. Tell me, Dr. Strangelove, why didn't you just do all of this in a laboratory and have farm animals brought in? You were out hunting dead bodies in the name of science?"

Mule cut in tentatively. "We were out hunting roadkill. The prof has ... principles."

"It was all a fortuitous bit of chance–our meeting–the bodies. You did us a favor, albeit a rather morbid one, and we will return that favor."

"By making us accomplices?" Delilah said.

Verdino blinked, honestly surprised. "You are the one who killed those people. If anything, we've made ourselves accomplices. You haven't heard us complaining about it."

"But what do we get from it?" Delilah asked. "When all of this is said and done, and you cart your ...test results...back to wherever it is you come from, what do Sam and I get?"

"You get closer to the border with a clean vehicle and identification that won't get you arrested or shot when you cross. We'll compensate you for your time and any help you provide. To me, that seems pretty fair."

Delilah leaned against the trailer, overcome, very suddenly, with laughter.

"Oh boy," she said. "And I said I was bored..."

"Let's get this wrapped up," Verdino said, ignoring Delilah's mirth, and the grins that were spreading across the faces of his crew. Bury anything we aren't taking with us and get the rest stowed. We should be out of here in less than an hour."

"Look," Amanda called out. They all turned. In the distance, they saw the T-Bird just coming back into sight.

TWENTY

Sam was making better time on the return trip. Terence sat beside him as they sent up twin rooster tails of dust in their wake. Then, glancing at the mirror to his right, Terence sat up straighter.

"Don't look now," he said, but we've got company. "I have to say–it doesn't look like Stone's people to me."

"What the hell?" Sam said. "Out here? What do you think they want?"

He glanced into the rear-view and saw two four wheel drive pickup trucks starting to close the gap behind them.

"Not sure," Terence said. "Either they're hoping we have beer, or they want trouble. That guy on the right has a shotgun."

Sam studied the trucks more carefully. There were two men in each, and just as Terence had warned him, one was dangling crazily out a passenger side window, trying to level a pretty large shotgun at the T-bird's back bumper.

"Sweet Christ," Sam said. "This just keeps getting better. Hold on."

He jammed his foot down on the accelerator, and the T-bird

roared, shooting across the rough terrain like it had been fired from a cannon.

Terence snapped out a cell phone and hit speed dial.

"Prof?" he said. "We have a problem. Not sure where they came from, but we have two pickups on our trail. Two passengers in each, armed and stupid."

He listened for a second, nodded, and flipped the phone closed.

"They'll be ready," he said.

"I hope to God they are," Sam said. "These clowns are starting to gain on us again. We've got the faster vehicle, but the T-bird isn't meant for this off-road crap. If we don't break an axle before we get back, it'll be a miracle. You might want to grab that sawed-off out from under the seat."

Terence didn't ask questions, just dragged the weapon free and gave it a quick once over.

"No safety?"

"Not meant for recreational shooting."

Sam hit the brakes and down-shifted, sliding in a quick 180 that lined the T-bird up with the front end of the trailer. The door was open, and Delilah stood in it, staring out at them with wild eyes. Terence and Sam dove out of the T-bird, slammed the doors, and ran for the trailer. As they went, Terence turned, staring back at the approaching trucks, the shotgun in his hand leveled.

"Who the hell is that?" Delilah asked, pointing at the approaching trucks, "and why are they chasing you?"

"Great questions," Sam said, gripping her by the waist and pushing her back inside. "I'll take a shot at answering them if you get the hell out of the door and let us in!"

Terence dove in behind him, and slammed the door. Outside,

the two trucks slowed, and began circling the trailer, engines revving.

...

Verdino stood calmly in the back corner of the trailer, his back to the others, talking on his cell phone. After a moment, he nodded and turned to the others.

"Help is on the way," he said. "All we have to do is stay locked up and wait."

"How far out are they?" Terence asked

"No more than an hour," Verdino said.

"You're kidding, right?" Delilah said. "You want us to try and hole up in here for an hour while those shit-heels pretend we're a wagon train? What if they decide to start shooting through the walls or the door, or take out the tires? What then?"

"Oh, I'm sure…"

"Screw that," Sam said.

He took the shotgun from Terence and went back to the door at the front of the trailer, opened it a crack, and looked out. One of the two trucks idled only a few yards away. The guy behind the wheel had the steering wheel in one hand and a beer in the other. His partner saw the open door and leveled the shotgun.

Sam shook his head.

"What the hell do you clowns want?" he called, fighting to be heard over the truck's engine.

"Don't rightly know that do we hoss?" the driver replied. "Don't know yet what you got. I know you're on our proppity."

"There's an 'r' in property," Sam said.

"Huh?"

"Listen," Sam went on, "we'll be out of here in an hour. We've got people coming. We didn't know we were on your land."

"Reckon if that's true, we'd best get in there and see what you got before the cavalry rides in, whatta ya say?"

"You don't want to do that," Sam said.

The driver drained his beer and tossed the can out the window. He never quit grinning.

"And why's that?"

Sam didn't hesitate. He leveled the sawed off shotgun and fired. The shot crashed through the center of the truck's windshield. There was a shower of blood and broken glass, and the truck slammed into reverse. Sam took a second shot, hit the back tire, and the truck–moving too quickly and not well controlled, tipped and rolled on its side.

"You didn't have to…" Verdino never got the words out.

"Hell he didn't," Delilah said.

She stepped to the back of the trailer, and before anyone could stop her, she slapped her palm into the switch that opened the rear door. She let it run, just long enough that there was a door sized crack to the right, and to the left.

"What the hell are you doing?" Kurt asked.

"Watch and learn, grasshopper," Delilah said. "Watch and learn."

She grabbed a jacket hanging from a hook on the wall and flipped it through the crack to the right side of the door. A furious burst of gunfire followed, and at that moment, Delilah dove out the left side, the gleaming .45 raised and ready. Mule stepped up and hit the switch to close the door.

"What the hell did you do that for?" Terence said.

"You don't want to get shot do you?" Mule asked.

"Christ," Terence said. He bent, pulled a small snub-nosed revolver out of his boot, and followed Sam out the front door.

"Wait here, then," he said. Then he was gone.

The others dropped low, keeping near the center of the trailer.

There was another burst of gunfire, then another, a small explosion… and then silence.

TWENTY-ONE

Goodman drove a little over the speed limit, keeping his eyes on the pavement ahead. He knew that if he pushed it, he'd eventually catch up. People running from the law would not be speeding any more than they had to–it attracted attention –and besides, they didn't really know anyone was following. Beside that, he was out of his jurisdiction, and he didn't know the roads as well as he'd have liked.

He saw an exit coming up. It read "Benson." He didn't know the place, but he was pretty certain it was too close to Peyote Slim's for their fugitives to hole up in. He ignored the exit and pressed on.

A few moments later, Brogan's cruiser passed the same point on the road. He also ignored the exit. About a mile past town, he saw something in the distance. It looked like a cloud of dust. Something was moving out on the desert. He slowed and saw a dirt road winding out into the distance.

He pulled over and grabbed his radio.

"FOURSTARSIX this is Brogan. You copy?"

"I got you," Goodman replied. "What's up?"

"Not sure. There's a side road here. I see some dust rising out over the desert. I'm gonna detour a bit, see if I can figure out what's out there. Might be nothing, but if our boys are trying something tricky…"

"Got it," Goodman said. "I'll see you on down the road."

"Brogan out."

He clipped the microphone onto the radio and turned off the highway, pointing the cruiser into the desert.

TWENTY-TWO

Outside the trailer, Terence and Delilah stood side by side, covering the one truck that remained upright. The other lay tipped over on its side, and Sam watched it cautiously to be sure it didn't explode.

As they waited, a hand slipped up through the passenger side window of the overturned truck. Then a second. The driver, still alive, but streaming blood from a cut on his scalp and moving as if in a daze, drew himself up and over his dead passenger. He slid through the window, bent at the waist, and then fell out and over the side of the truck into the dirt. A small cloud of dust rose as he hit, and for a moment he lay very still. Then he reached out and pushed his palm to the ground as if to lift himself up.

Terence ignored him and moved over to the upright truck slowly, covering it as he went.

Delilah approached the guy on the ground and kicked him in the rib, dropping him back to the dirt.

"Hold it right there," she said. "You don't want to join your friend in the truck, you'll show me what a pretty statue you can be."

"The other two didn't make it," Terence called from over by the second truck.

"What a shame," Delilah said. She didn't lower her gun from the one redneck still moving.

"Don't kill him," Sam said. "I have an idea."

"A fun idea?" Delilah asked, turning, and winking at him.

"Freak," Sam said. "No, a *good* idea, if it works. I think our new buddy here can actually do us a favor."

"You have to be kidding," Delilah said.

Sam ignored her. He walked over to where the man lay in the dirt, bent, and grabbed him by the arm.

"Get up," he said.

He hauled on the arm, and the man did as he was told, staggering as he gained his footing. Sam placed the barrel of the sawed off shotgun against his temple.

"What's your name?" he said.

"Cl-Clarence," the man answered.

"One, or two 'C's?" Sam asked.

"Clarence," Delilah said. She rolled the name off her lips a second time. "Clarence. Christ, that sounds like the name of a cow in a kid's book. You can't be serious."

Sam shook him. "Clarence, you hear me? You understand me?"

Clarence nodded. He didn't look too steady on his feet, but his eyes had gone from dazed to scared shitless and he leaned as far from the touch of the shotgun barrel as he could without falling down again.

"Terence, get the Prof out here, would you?" Sam asked. "I want to run something by him." Then he turned back to his prisoner.

"Tell me, C-Clarence…can you drive a stick?"

A moment later, Verdino followed Terence out of the trailer.

He stood beside Sam, ignoring Clarence, and took in the scene with obvious disapproval.

"Well, this is a mess," he said.

"Yeah, well, we had to improvise." Delilah said. "You know… spur of the moment planning never works out like you hope…"

"I think I have an idea, Prof," Sam said, "but you'd better get your boys busy on those bodies. Whatever we do, we can't leave them lying around. What do we do…just chop them up and drop them in the soup?"

Verdino turned and stared at him. The corner of his mouth twitched as if he might smile.

"Something like that," he said.

Delilah snorted and turned away, shaking her head.

"You better get them started," Sam said. "Meanwhile, I think old Clarence here has decided to cooperate with us, haven't you Clarence?"

Clarence nodded, still not speaking.

"Let me tell you what I think about old Clarence, Prof."

This time, Verdino did smile. "I'm all ears," he said.

TWENTY-THREE

Brogan drove slowly out into the desert, watching the horizon for any sign of movement. He hadn't seen any more dust plumes for a while, but he had a good idea which direction they'd come from. He didn't plan on turning back until he found sign of what had caught his eye in the first place.

Then he slowed and stopped.

In the distance, coming straight at him, and moving fast, a single rooster tail of dust rose into the sky. He stared, trying to make out exactly what, and in that short span of a few moments, a red blur materialized out of the desert. It was the Porsche, and it was moving like a bat out of hell, straight at him.

"Christ," he said. He put the cruiser in reverse and gunned the engine. Even so, he barely cleared the side of the road when the Porsche blew past him. It was moving so fast the driver was nothing but a blur.

Brogan glanced a last time into the desert, slammed his hand on the wheel, and dropped the cruiser back into gear.

"I'll be god damned," he said. He shot off back toward the freeway in hopeless pursuit of the Porsche, flipping on his lights and hitting the siren. If anyone was out there, they'd know he'd been close, but he had no choice. He couldn't afford to let anyone escape.

"Damn," he grated.

The Porsche was nothing but a trail of floating dust as he shot down the road after it, praying the idiot would hit a pothole or a rock before he reached the open highway. It didn't seem possible the car could be moving so fast.

❞❞❞

Verdino stood very still. He was gazing after the Porsche with a pair of high-powered binoculars. After a moment he lowered them, turned, and smiled.

"That was good timing," he said. "It seems our new friend just dragged a local sheriff off our trail."

"I hope ol' Clarence can drive," Delilah said. "That County-Mountie catches him too quick, he might come back to see where he started from."

"He won't catch the Porsche," Amanda said. "It's not standard. Daddy made some…modifications."

Delilah turned to stare at her.

"I have *got* to meet this father of yours. Is he married?"

Sam whacked her on the arm, and everyone laughed.

"All right then," Verdino said. "Let's get this over with."

The two pickup trucks both stood upright, and with a bit of hammering and cursing, Sam and Terence had gotten them both running. The bodies were gone; Kurt and Mule were stripping off green rubber gloves and aprons.

"There's a canyon not too far past where we dropped off the cab to the truck," Terence said. "I say we take these bad boys and drop them right on in."

"I'm in," Sam said. He grinned like a schoolboy. "I always

wanted to do that, jump out of a car at the last minute and watch it dive off the cliff. Just like in a bad "B" movie."

"Just like," Terence said.

"I'll follow in the T-bird," Delilah said. "You two stunt-man heroes will be needing a ride back."

Before they could take off, the silence was broken by the sound of approaching engines. They all turned to the south. A small caravan of sleek black vehicles rolled steadily toward them. The drivers were careful to raise as little smoke as possible, and as they drew near, they veered off, some heading to where the group stood, others breaking off to different tasks. They were a well-oiled machine, and it wasn't until he saw the driver of a new truck cab begin to back toward the trailer that Terence sprang into action. He ran to the truck, waving his hands.

"Hold on there," he called. "Ain't no one hooking up that rig but me, so you climb right on out of there Jimmy!"

The driver grinned, saluted, and brought the truck to a halt. He climbed down, and moments later Terence was in and rolling slowly back toward the trailer, the two of them caught up in the job at hand.

An Italian man, immaculate in a tailored suit, dark glasses, and perfectly groomed hair stepped from one of the sedans and crossed over to where Verdino stood, waiting.

"Paisano," Verdino said. "I'm flattered. I didn't expect Mr. Stone to be sending you."

"Mr. Stone says you have some problems. Making problems go away is my specialty. What is the situation?"

"For starters, we need these two trucks, and that T-bird to go away," Verdino said.

Paisano nodded, but before he could speak, Sam cut in.

"Wait just a minute. What do you mean the T-bird? That's my car!"

Paisano turned to him, pulled off his shades, and grinned. His teeth were perfect, smooth, white, and gleaming.

"You must be Sam," he said. "I brought you a trade. I think you'll be alright with it."

"I hope you don't mind," Verdino said. "I was afraid you might be too attached to the car, so I arranged for something special…"

Sam turned to the line of cars and studied them. At the end of the line, tucked in behind the last of the identical sedans, he caught a glimmer of chrome. Slowly, he left the group and walked over to where he could see more clearly.

What he saw was a perfectly restored, 1966 Oldsmobile Toronado. It looked as if it had just been driven off the showroom floor.

Delilah stepped up beside him and whistled softly.

"All it needs is the bumper sticker," she said.

Sam turned to her. "What in the hell are you going on about?"

"You know," she said, nodding at the car. "Like in that Stephen King movie? It's the same car. Should say 'High Toned Son of a Bitch'–sounds about right."

Sam opened the door and slid in behind the wheel, running his hands over the upholstery. He turned and grinned up at Delilah.

"You," he said, "are seriously strange."

"Keep complimenting me like that and you might get lucky," she said.

"Already am."

* * *

Paisano's crew was fast, efficient, and attentive to detail. Terence had the trailer hooked up and the engine running. Kurt and Mule sealed up the trailer, secured their equipment and readied things for the road. Sam and Delilah moved their few belongings to the Toronado, then the trucks and T-bird disappeared into the distance.

"Where's my car?" Amanda asked.

"Your father said you could take any of them you liked," Paisano said. He nodded at the sedans.

Amanda stared at the sleek anonymous vehicles, hands on her hips, and then glanced over at the Toronado. She smiled and turned.

"No thank you," she said. "I think I'll ride with them."

"Are you sure, darling?" Verdino asked.

"I'll be fine, Gregory. You get in your truck and try to keep up."

Sam and Delilah turned to stare at one another, then Delilah cracked up.

"Of course," she said.

Sam got out, held the door, and tipped the seat forward so Amanda could climb in back."

"That's settled, then," Verdino said.

Paisano nodded deferentially.

"There's a road about a mile off," he said, pointing south. "It curves back to the highway. You should be safe once you reach that."

"Thank you," Verdino said.

The two men shook hands, and a few moments later, the truck, dragging its completely re-surfaced trailer, rolled away from the small rocky crag. Behind it, the Toronado bounced and rumbled, following as close as was safe. When Sam glanced in his rearview a few moments later, it was as if Paisano, the sedans and men, had never been there at all.

TWENTY-FOUR

oodman drove steadily south, watching the desert to either side. There was no sign of Brogan. He reached down and grabbed the microphone of his radio.

"Brogan, you out there? Where'd you go? Over."

After only a moment, the radio crackled.

"I'm in pursuit of our Porsche. That's one hot automobile, my friend. I clocked it at 160 mph, and it pulled away. I radioed ahead to try and get some help to cut him off, but I don't know."

"Christ," Goodman said. "No sign of the truck, or the T-Bird?"

"Not this way. There was something going on out on the desert, but I didn't get a chance to check it out. Guess you're on your own for now. I'm sticking with this until I get him or lose him for good."

"Good luck, then," Goodman said. "I'll keep moving, and we can hook up on down the road. Keep me posted."

"You got it. Brogan out."

The radio went silent, and Goodman popped the microphone back onto its hook. Headlights had appeared in his rear-view, and he slowed slightly, watching as they approached. It only took a moment to see that it was a big rig, and Goodman felt his heartbeat speed slightly.

Then the distance closed, and the long, dark form of the truck slid into the left-hand lane and rolled slowly past. It was gray, not green, worn and scuffed. He frowned and shook his head. Not their guys.

Then, as the truck crossed back in front of him, he caught another set of lights in the mirror. The car was low-slung and dark, and for just a second, he thought it was going to be the T-bird. Then it passed him as well, as if hurrying to catch up to the truck. It was a mint condition, 1966 Oldsmobile Toronado.

"No freakin' way," he said softly.

He reached for the microphone again, had it in his hand ready to key the mic, and then dropped it back into place with another quick shake of his head. He pressed his foot to the gas pedal and shot down the road in pursuit of the Toronado."

"Brogan, ol' buddy," he said. "I hope one of us is on the right trail."

. . .

Sam drove the Toronado carefully at the speed limit. He glanced into the mirror for about the tenth time, cursing under his breath. Delilah sat beside him, staring into the passenger side mirror. Behind them, Amanda sat, turned with her face pressed to the rear window.

"It's the same one," Amanda said at last.

"Same what?" Sam asked.

"That State Trooper back there," she said. "His cruiser has a big scrape on the rear left fender. I just remembered where I've seen it before. It was on TV–during the report on the Sunny-Side-Up Diner. Gregory said…"

"You have to be kidding me," Delilah cut her off. "You're

telling me you can remember a scrape on the side of a car well enough to recognize it?"

"I notice things, particularly about cars. That cruiser has a four speed automatic tranny with a 4.6 Liter 16-valve V8. It can fly, and he isn't taking care of it. I have a thing about big engines…"

Sam started laughing.

"You have *got* to be freakin' kidding me," Delilah repeated.

"Nope," Amanda said. "Sixteen valves. Really."

"Christ," Sam said. "Next you'll tell me you have a cousin named Vinny. See if you can get Gregory on the phone, will you … *darling*? You might want to let him know what you saw, because if that is the *same* trooper, it's no coincidence he's driving down this road. It's a long way from his usual stomping grounds."

"Don't' tell me you believe her?" Delilah said, turning to scowl at Sam in disbelief.

"Well," Sam drawled, "I wasn't really sure, cupcake, but I think I'm starting to be a believer."

Delilah and Amanda turn to see what Sam has already caught in the rear-view. The cruiser, which had dropped back after they passed it, was now coming up fast. It was not flashing lights, but it was closing in.

"He can't know who we are," Delilah said. "The truck, the car, they're not the same."

"Maybe, maybe not," Sam said. "Amanda honey, you better get 'Gregory' on the phone and let him know what's going on. See what he wants us to do."

Amanda turned around, grabbed her phone, and dialed.

After a moment, she smiled.

"Yes, Gregory honey, I love you too. Listen, we have a problem…"

TWENTY-FIVE

In the truck, Terence, like Sam, watched his speed carefully.

"I hate Troopers," he said. "Sometimes, they get bored on a lonely night. Sometimes they pull you over just to talk. Just in case."

Helen was quiet, but she looked worried. Professor Verdino was leaning in from the trailer. He had his phone pressed tightly to his ear. He spoke softly for a moment or two, and then hung up.

"That trooper is on our tail," he said. "I don't think he's decided whether to try pulling us over. He's alone. Amanda says it's the same cruiser that was all the way back at the Sunny-Side-Up. If so, this is one of the officers that investigated the first killings."

"You think she's right?" Terence asked, obviously skeptical. "That's a long way to follow, and why would he be alone?"

"I've doubted her a few times," Verdino said. "Every time, it's ended badly."

"Maybe we should just let him catch us," Helen said slowly.

"What do you mean," Verdino asked.

"If he's really alone, and there's no backup, we might be able to keep him away from his radio."

"And do what?" Terence asked. "I'm down for almost anything, but I didn't sign on to kill any Trooper."

"No one is getting killed," Verdino said. "At least, not if we can help it. We have to find a way to get him off our trail without giving away our identities, assuming he's chasing us at all. With the addition of the bodies of those unfortunate–*gentlemen*–who accosted us back down the road, we're very close to having enough raw material to complete our work. We are on the verge of a working formula. Whether or not this is the same trooper, we can't afford to have him pull us over and search the trailer."

"That all sounds great," Terence said. "Let me know if you figure it out. Meanwhile, I'm keeping the speed at fifty-five and the nose pointed toward the gulf."

"I'm going to call Mr. Stone," Verdino said. "Whatever we do, it should be his call."

Verdino dialed his phone, waited, and then spoke.

"Mr. Stone, Gregory here sir."

"I figured you'd call," Stone's clipped, non-nonsense voice replied. "You seem to have something of a problem, Gregory. Good thing I've had my boys keeping tabs on you."

"Sir?"

"They've been paralleling you on a country road. I'd say it's only a matter of time before that Trooper on your tail decides to pull you over and check his hunch."

"I..."

"Just listen, Gregory, you don't have all that much time. I'm not letting you drag my money, or my daughter, through the legal system. Not to mention the time and equipment. In exactly five minutes, I'm sending in a diversion. I expect you to take full advantage of it. Are we clear?"

Verdino started to answer but stopped as the line went dead. He stared at the phone, then quickly started dialing.

"Amanda, darling," he said. "I just spoke with your father. It seems he's been keeping an eye on us, and he's sending in more help. Could you please tell Sam to expect something–unexpected–in the next five minutes?"

He hesitated, shook his head, and smiled.

"No, I don't know what it is."

Another hesitation, and then "Yes, dear, I love you too."

"What's going on?" Terence asked tersely.

"I have no idea, I'm afraid," Verdino answered, but I know that–whatever it is–we have five minutes."

TWENTY-SIX

Goodman's mind was whirling. It was obviously not the same truck, and a Toronado is worlds away from a T-bird, but the combination. It was just too strange to be a coincidence. He thought again about calling Brogan, but if he was wrong, he might divert the other man from a real suspect. Instead, he leaned down and reached for the button to flip on his siren. Then, just before his finger brushed the switch, another set of headlights rushed up from behind.

He sat back and stared into the rear-view in disbelief. Coming up fast, chrome glinting in the moonlight, was the black T-bird. He thought he recognized the driver, and there was a long-haired woman sitting beside him. The car drew up so close behind him he thought they would strike his bumper.

"What the hell?" Goodman muttered.

Then, the woman in the T-bird, leaned up close to the windshield, winked at him, and flipped him the bird. Just about that time, the driver braked, put the car into a skid, performed the slickest high-speed 180 that Goodman had ever seen in or out of a movie, and tore off back down the road the way they'd come.

"I'll be God Damned," Goodman said. He stomped on the brakes. He wasn't ready for the maneuver, and for just a moment he felt his tires leaving the pavement, felt the gravity shift. Then he – and the cruiser – dropped back onto the road. The tires caught, and he came to a full stop pointed north, and took off after the T-Bird, sirens wailing.

...

Verdino had his phone to his ear again. He listened for a moment, and then hung up.

"Well?" Terence said.

"He fell for it. They've bought us some time. We need to move fast. You're going to have to get us off this highway and find another route."

"It won't be smooth," Terence said, "but there's a crossroad in a few miles. If we take that, we can hit the older state road, and turn back south."

"Perfect," Verdino said. He turned then and ducked back into the trailer. Terence put the pedal to the metal and roared into the darkness.

Verdino closed the portal between the cab and the trailer. He leaned back against it heavily.

After a moment, Mule walked over to him.

"Hey, Professor…"

"Yes," Verdino said, regaining his poise.

"The last batch was bigger than we thought. We did pretty well. I think…unless we get a bulimic model…one more body would do it. We could take the process to the next stage."

Verdino walked past Mule and headed for the equipment consoles. He twisted one of the monitors up so he could view it better, and began typing, checking gauges and sensors. He worked for a moment or two, and then stepped back, turning to Mule.

"You are right, of course. One more. One more body and we can return to the lab. I thought we'd have to make off with several bodies from the flood. Now I wonder if we should even wait."

"What do you mean?" Kurt asked, looking up from where he'd been reading in the corner.

Verdino didn't answer. He returned to the front of the trailer, opened the hatch into the compartment behind the driver's seat, and stepped through. He closed the door behind him without looking back.

. . .

Brogan slowed the cruiser, banged his hand on the steering wheel, and pulled off the freeway. The Porsche had turned off onto a side road and shot out into the desert. There was no way he was catching up with it.

He'd called in a few minutes earlier and air support would arrive soon, but somehow, he thought they were going to find nothing much waiting for them. He leaned in and grabbed his microphone, watching the trail of dust from the departing Porsche in disgust.

"FOURSTARSIX–this is Brogan. You copy?"

After a moment, the radio crackled and Goodman's voice shot back, short and terse.

"Can't talk. You aren't going to believe this, but I'm in pursuit of the damned T-Bird."

"I lost the Porsche," Brogan said. "That thing runs like a bat out of hell."

"You might as well join me, then," Goodman said. "I'm headed your way, fast, and the T-bird is caught between."

"You got it," Brogan said. He dropped the mic back onto its

holder, climbed back behind the wheel and did another U-Turn, heading south.

TWENTY-SEVEN

It was many hours later, and Terence directed the big rig down a narrow, bumpy country road. He couldn't get up much speed, but they'd been off the freeway for quite some time, and were currently running by moonlight, so pursuit, at this point, didn't seem too likely. He concentrated on keeping them on the road and maintaining what speed he could.

In the rearview, he saw the Toronado cruising along behind.

The door between the trailer and the cab opened, and Professor Verdino clambered through, seating himself in a crew seat behind Helen and staring out into the night.

"Taking a little shortcut, Prof," Terence said. "We'll hit another state road in an hour or so and turn back south."

"How does it affect our time to the gulf?" Verdino asked.

"Not making it tonight. I figured we'd get as far out here as we could, then pull over and out of sight to camp. They're probably still looking for us, but I doubt they'll make it out this far. You think they'll catch those two in the T-Bird?"

"If they do," Verdino sighed, "I'm sure I'll hear all about the legal fees incurred. They won't be able to pin anything on them–the car is clean now, and there's nothing to tie the driver or his passenger to any of the killings. They could just claim someone sold them the car for fifty bucks and they were out joy-riding. Nothing to link them to us now, either."

"One thing I've learned," Terence said, keeping his eyes carefully on the road. "The police are almost never as stupid as you think they are. I wouldn't count them out too quickly, and we'd better not let our guard down."

"Indeed," Verdino said. "If only our luck had held a little longer…"

"What do you mean?" Terence asked.

"Mule tells me we're only a single body from completing our work. We started out looking at a much longer timeframe, hoping to pick up road kill, or hook up with some hunters. The human remains are larger, and we've been able to process them fairly quickly."

"You suggestin' that people burn better?" Terence asked.

"So it would seem."

"You wouldn't be thinking about finding someone to shoot and top off the tank, would you? Said a couple of times already that I'm not signed on for that."

"No, of course not," Verdino said. "But…"

"Wait," Terence said, cutting him off. "What the hell is that?"

Off to the right side of the road, a black SUV had flipped over several times, ending up on its roof. Smoke rolled from the engine compartment, and flames licked at the far side of the vehicle.

"Pull over," Verdino said. "Quickly! I want to see if we can help!"

"Help?" Terence said. He pulled slowly over to the side of the road, careful not to drop his front tire into the ditch.

Verdino turned and climbed back through into the trailer, closing the door behind him.

"I got a bad feeling about this," Helen said, staring at the door.

"You and me both," Terence said. He opened his door and clambered down to the road.

The door on the side of the trailer burst open. Kurt, Mule, and Verdino piled out, jumped the ditch, and ran toward the burning vehicle. Sam, Delilah, and Amanda were right behind them.

As they closed in on the SUV, they could see that there was a second vehicle–a beat up old black pickup truck with the front end completely caved in–off to the side.

"They must have hit almost head on," Sam called out. "Looks like the SUV tried to turn–didn't quite make it."

"Kurt, Mule, Terence, check out the fire–don't get too close. It's been burning for a while. They may have been thrown free or crawled out."

"We're checking the truck?" Sam said.

"Seems like the best bet for survivors," Verdino said. "It's damaged, but at least it's not on fire. Could be survivors."

"What if it there are?" Sam said. "Survivors are kind of a problem, aren't they? I mean, at this point in time it wouldn't be a great idea for us to be dragging accident victims into the Emergency Room."

"We can't just leave them here, can we? It would be better to chance running someone into a hospital than to call from out here and alert the authorities to our location–assuming they're still after us."

"Oh, they're after us," Sam said. As soon as they figure out the people in the Porsche and the T-Bird are there to distract them, they'll be back out here, scouring the countryside, towns, and back roads for us. It's what they do."

"Yes...but I've been thinking about that." Verdino said, fighting for breath as he hurried to keep up with the others. "It seems as if the two officers are following us on their own. I think they might be almost as reluctant to call in and tell their superiors that they believe they've been on the trail of mass murderers but let them slip away and never called for backup as we are to be caught."

"You might have a point, at that," Sam said. "Better two than a posse, I guess."

Sam reached the truck first. He leaned in and wiped dirt off the driver's side window.

"We have something here," he said.

He grabbed the handle on the door and heaved, but nothing happened. He tried again, but the door wouldn't budge.

Verdino hurried to the far side, reached down, and grabbed the passenger side door. He pulled, and it groaned, then, with a quick snap that almost threw him on his ass, it opened.

"We have one body," he said. "The driver."

"Alive?" Sam called.

"I can't tell yet. Someone get over here and help me get him out."

Sam ran to help, and in moments they had carefully dragged the man free. He was young, probably in his early twenties. Verdino knelt at his side and placed a finger to his throat.

"He's alive," he said. "The pulse is there, fairly strong."

"Don't know whether to curse or say 'Yay!'" Sam said.

Before Verdino could reply, Kurt, who had been at the SUV with Terence and Mule, let out a scream.

"Look out!" he called.

The night erupted in a bright explosion of fire and smoke. Verdino turned toward the SUV and was slammed back against the ruined truck. Sam dropped to the ground, covering the body of the driver reflexively as dirt and debris rained down on them.

Verdino recovered first. He pushed up off of the truck and stumbled toward the source of the explosion.

"Kurt!" he cried. "Mule!"

There was no answer.

"Sam," he said, "get him out of here. I'm going to try and reach the others."

He turned without waiting for an answer and disappeared into the smoke. Sam cursed under his breath. He grabbed the wounded man under the arms and began dragging him unceremoniously toward the road. As he went, he saw Terence, stumbling along the edge of the smoke from the explosion. A moment later, Verdino staggered out, dragging Mule by one arm. Seconds later, Kurt crawled free, and Terence hurried to help the younger man to his feet.

"Jesus. There were two people in there," Mule choked out. "Two older guys. I saw some kind of whiskey bottle broken on the dashboard. I was gonna try and get them out ..."

"They weren't coming out of that any way but a pine box," Terence said. "Let it go."

"Hey," Sam called. "A little help over here!"

Terence left Kurt and hurried over to help Sam. Between the two of them they half dragged, half carried the young man to the side of the road, where Delilah and Helen stood waiting.

"Is he alive?" Delilah asked.

"Yeah, last time we checked," Sam said. "Why, is that a problem?"

"Not sure," Delilah said. "We aren't exactly in the life *saving* business these days."

"Well, we couldn't just leave him there," Verdino said. "Hurry up and get him into the trailer. We need to get moving. I don't think we've left any real evidence of our presence here, but that smoke is going to attract attention. We'll want to be far away before someone investigates."

"I can see the news story now," Helen said. "Another bizarre story in the desert–two vehicles in an apparent collision, one burns, the other's driver seems to have climbed out and walked away without a trace."

"Swell," Terence muttered.

Sam and Terence carried the man into the trailer. Kurt held the door, and Mule cleared off one of the benches so there was room to lay him out.

"Sit with him," Verdino said. "Make sure he doesn't roll off onto the floor."

"What do we do if he wakes up?" Mule asked.

"Keep him still. Tell him we're taking him to the hospital."

"Are we?" Kurt said.

"I suppose that remains to be seen," Verdino said. He turned and left the trailer. Terence and Sam followed.

As Sam and Delilah made their way back to the Toronado, Amada, who had remained in the backseat waiting, glanced up. She was doing her nails.

"What happened?" she asked.

"Pat yourself on the back," Sam said, climbing in behind the wheel. "We're heroes."

Amanda smiled and went back to her nails.

"I always knew that Gregory would do good work," she said.

Laughing, Delilah dropped into the passenger side seat and reclined it, putting her feet up on the dash.

Moments later, the truck pulled back onto the road, and the Toronado followed, leaving the flames and the wreckage behind.

TWENTY-EIGHT

Kurt and Mule stood to the side and watched the man they'd rescued, as the truck rolled steadily off into the distance. Verdino stepped forward and leaned in, checking the man's pulse.

"What do you think, Prof?" Kurt asked.

"Too early to say for sure, but there are no broken bones, and he's breathing well enough. He's suffered a nasty crack to the head."

"I'll say," Mule said. "Look at the size of that lump."

Just then, the man groaned, and Verdino stepped back.

"Looks like he's coming around," Kurt said.

"Is that good…or bad?" Mule asked.

The man's eyes fluttered, then opened. He blinked, took in Kurt, Mule, Verdino, and all the glistening, metallic equipment behind them. His eyes opened wider, and he began to struggle, pulling against the straps holding him in place wildly.

"No," he screamed. "No, don't do it man, don't…"

Verdino held up his hands.

"Young man, calm down," he said. "No one is going to…"

"Don't probe me, man! I'll talk! I'll tell you anything you want to know. Don't...don't probe me."

Kurt glanced at Mule, who grinned back at him.

"Dude thinks we're aliens," he said.

Mule leaned in, very quickly, waved his hands in front of the man's eyes, and said "Boo!"

Verdino pushed him aside roughly.

"That will be quite enough of that," he said. "Young man, no one is going to–probe you. We are not aliens. We are scientists. You were in an accident."

"An accident? Where am I?"

"I'm afraid that is going to be a very long story," Verdino said. "Are you in any pain? Can we get you anything?"

"I could use a drink."

Mule walked to the small refrigerator at the end of the trailer and retrieved a bottle of water, holding it out.

"You're gonna have to find something stronger than that," the man said. "Seriously, what's that green shit over there? Acid?"

"Dude," Kurt said, "What's your name? I'm Kurt."

"Sully. They call me Sully. It's short for...well...maybe you untie me?"

"Of course," Verdino said. "We just didn't want you to roll off the bench. And Kurt, I believe we still have some bourbon?"

"You got it, prof. It's in the cabinet over by the...still."

Verdino leaned down and unfastened the straps.

"You'll want to sit up slowly," Verdino said. "You were in a bad accident, and I'm a professor, not a doctor of medicine. I don't believe anything is broken, but you can't be too careful."

Sully sat up very slowly, rubbing the back of his neck.

"Hey," he said. "I just woke up in a spaceship. I'll be taking everything slow. Except maybe that bourbon."

"You might want a double," Mule said. "This story is a doozy."

"Hell," Sully said with a grin, taking the drink Kurt offered, "at least I didn't get probed."

. . .

They pulled into the parking lot of the Whispering Pines Motel, rolling in slowly to take in their surroundings. There were a dozen or so units in a line like a run-down strip mall. The office window was dusted over, but a dim light shone from within, and a neon sign above it blinked VAC N Y to the night.

There was a U-haul trailer parked outside one of the units.

"There," Verdino said.

Mule pulled in beside the trailer, and they climbed out. Verdino worked the combination lock on the rear of the trailer and slid the doors open.

"Paisano came through. Everything is here. We have clothing we can wear to blend in with the volunteers at the flood site. We have flashlights and equipment."

Sam stepped up and eyed the truck's contents warily.

"I don't know, Prof," he said. "It just doesn't feel right. I mean, sure, in theory it's simple–hundreds of volunteers, every different agency the government has in one big cluster, stepping on one another's feet and all, but it still feels like walking into a trap."

"He's right, you know," Delilah said. "There are too many variables. There will be police, Coast Guard, National Guard, and a lot of others, but all it takes is one slip–one time someone makes a body count, and it doesn't add up. Just waltzing in and back out with dead bodies is probably a lot more complicated than it sounds, and we still have those two jokers on our trail."

"'Scuse me," Sully cut in, "but let me get this straight. Your plan is to walk into a flood zone, join the rescue party and then walk back out with a dead body or two? I gotta wonder why you'd do that? I mean, not that I'm a fella who steals bodies on a regular basis, but why not just take 'em from the morgue? I mean, if they're hauling them out of the gulf, they gotta be takin' them somewhere, right?"

Verdino stood very still, thinking.

"You're right, of course. Not sure why I didn't think of that. They're going to be piled up, and there are going to be a lot more dead than they are used to dealing with. No reason to chance mucking about in a swollen river and drawing attention."

"This just keeps getting better," Delilah said. "From public servant rescuer to morgue robber in less than an hour. My mother would be so proud."

"Like she's dancing in the street now," Sam said.

"Let's get into the rooms and unpacked," Verdino said. "I really think we're onto something here–something that could simplify and speed our progress considerably. Let's settle, and then I want you all to come to my room for a strategy meeting. I believe we may need to send out a scouting party."

Without further discussion they closed the trailer, emptied the trunk of the Toronado, and entered three of the run-down motel rooms, Sam and Delilah in one, Verdino and Amanda in another, Mule, Kurt and Sully in the last.

TWENTY-NINE

Goodman stood beside his cruiser, pulled off to the edge of the freeway. The road was empty as far as he could see in either direction. He leaned on the front fender, smacked a cigarette from the pack, and lit it. The landscape around him was flat and barren, scrub and rock, desert, and sand.

A moment later, headlights glowed on the skyline, and then faded from milky white dots to brilliant beams. Brogan slowed as he approached and pulled in behind Goodman. He got out and walked over. Goodman offered a smoke, and Brogan took it.

"So, you get the son of a bitch?" Goodman asked.

"I did," Brogan said. "Suspect is on his way to county, not talking. The car is on its way to impound. Got something else, though. Not sure what use it will be. Thought I'd run it by you and see if anything clicked."

"Let's have it then.

"Fella out in the desert called in earlier. He has a radio setup. Reckon you'd call him a nut job, given most circumstances. Lives in an old Airstream coated in tinfoil. Has antennas and radios of all description, mostly pointed at the stars."

"Tell me you're not going to say we're chasing a truck full of aliens…"

"Why…you worried about gettin' probed, or something?"

"Okay, okay. What did this guy find?"

"Didn't find anything. Heard something though. Seems, among other things, he can pick up cell phone conversations. I'll be going back to talk to him about that, at some point, but this time he caught something that might be of use. It was garbled, but he heard someone talking about a truck, something about bodies, and something about a flood."

Goodman cocked his head. "There's a flood at the Gulf right now."

"That's what I was thinking. I was also thinking, if we want to prevent more mysteriously missing bodies, we'd better get our tails in gear."

"I'll phone in. For the record? I'm telling them I have a friend down there reported lost in the flood. Gonna volunteer my services to help in the rescue operation."

"So.you aren't calling the rest of this in?"

"Are you?"

"Can't see how that could be good for my career. On the other hand, we find these clowns…"

"Or aliens?"

"Right. Either way, could look pretty good."

"In for a dollar then," Goodman said. "I reckon we'd better hit the road."

THIRTY

Kurt, Mule, Sam, Delilah, Sully, and Verdino stretched out in a line leading back into a darkened alley. The name of the town was Denzel, Texas. There was no one in sight, and the alley provided the rear entrances to a several businesses. Dumpsters lined the walls, and old bottles and cans littered the ground. They'd cruised the few downtown streets, found an all-night convenience store, and somehow managed to get directions to the morgue without drawing suspicion. The lights were still on inside, you could see the glow from the street, though the sign on the door had read CLOSED. Finding the alley in back had been a particularly good stroke of luck.

Sam, who was in the lead, reached out and grabbed hold of one of the doorknobs. The others stood very, very still. He turned the knob and pushed. It started to swing open, and Verdino stepped forward, grabbing his arm.

"Wait," he said. "Did you tell Amanda to keep the motor running?"

"Of course. Just because I'm crazy enough to go morgue-robbing at midnight doesn't mean I'm stupid."

Verdino nodded. They were all on edge, and it wasn't going to do them any good to quarrel.

"Alright then," he said. "Delilah, you and I will go in first."

"Um—why?" Delilah asked, not happy.

"I can pass myself off as a doctor, coming in from the flood. They're going to be confused. You are the most attractive and initially the least threatening. I'm counting on you not to live up to that."

Delilah cocked her head to one side, then chuckled. "Let me get this straight," she said. "You want me because I'm cute?"

"And dangerous," Sam said. Then he laughed. "That's why *I* want you."

"Can we try to focus?" Verdino said.

They all laughed then, and it broke some of the tension. Mule stepped up to hold the door, and Verdino entered, followed closely by Delilah, who regardless of her good humor, kept a hand near the butt of the .45.

"How long do we wait?" Mule said.

"Don't know about you," Sam said. "I'm in it for the long haul. I'll wait here until they come back for us, or I hear someone scream."

"This sucks," Kurt said. "I almost wish we'd gone to volunteer in the flood."

Sully leaned up to try and glance past them through the doorway.

"No way man. That Gulf water's fulla stuff you don't want anything to do with. Besides, I *been* on them volunteer missions. They got eyes in the back'a their heads. Volunteers steal stuff... they watch pretty close. Don't know if they'd watch bodies... never met no one out to *steal* bodies. Trust me, though, this is better."

Sam shook his head. "You're bat shit crazy. Better? This is

better? Really? Personally, I was thinking that if it hadn't been for the last two days of my life, I'd sure as hell have ranked this as the craziest-assed thing I'd ever done."

A sudden crash from inside silenced them. A moment later, Delilah poked her head out.

"If you guys are done chatting," she said, "You need to get in here. We have a situation."

She disappeared back inside, and they all followed, slipping into the morgue, and letting the door close them off from the alley, and from easy escape.

"Swell," Sam muttered. "Just freaking swell."

The morgue was about what they'd expected, a couple of deep sinks, worktables, lockers, and a small bank of drawers meant to hold the dead of a small town. That wasn't all, though. The place was overrun with bodies. They were stacked on gurneys, two and tree deep on the autopsy tables, shrouded and drenched in shadows. It was an eerie sight, like something out of a horror movie, and the air was close and thick with the scent of chemicals.

Professor Verdino stood in the middle of the room, glancing about himself calmly. Beside him stood Delilah, and beside Delilah, a girl. She was maybe twenty–blonde, petite, and crying. As they all stepped closer, they saw why.

On the floor, a man lay prone in a pool of blood.

Sully stepped forward for a better look. "Who's that?" he said.

The girl answered, fighting to control herself. "Ed," she said. "Ed Santos."

Verdino cut in. "It seems Mr. Santos is–or was–the Senior Morgue Attendant. I believe he's become his own next customer."

"My name is Rebecca," the girl said, "Rebecca Riley. Folks call me Becca for short. I came to talk to Mr. Santos about a job. He asked me to stop by at night–said there'd be more time for the interview. He didn't say he was interviewing on the couch in the lounge."

"Here?" Mule said, incredulous. "Here? He was…"

Becca ignored him. "When I tried to leave, he grabbed me. I hit him."

"With what?" Kurt asked.

Delilah grinned. She tossed a hammer up in the air. It flipped once, and then she caught it. Droplets of blood flew in glittering arcs from the metal head.

"Seems like ol' Eddy here was putting up some art in his office," she said.

"Sort of a hanging and banging night he had in mind, then?" Sam said.

"Exactly," Delilah said. "He should have put all his tools away."

As if just noticing she was among strangers, and that strange barely cut it, Becca backed away from Delilah.

"Who are you people?" she said. "Why are you here?"

"Strange you should ask," Verdino said. "The reason we're here has just changed. We were going to pick something up, but I think–considering the circumstances–we'd better help you out first. Kurt, bring in one of the bags. Let's get Mr. Santos out of here and things a little cleaner before someone else shows up."

"But what are you going to do?" Becca asked.

Delilah laughed out loud. "Honey, believe me when I tell you, you would not believe it, and you do not want to know. I was you? I'd hit the street and keep on going and forget I ever had an interview for this job. Maybe if you apply next week, the person in charge won't be such an asshole."

Becca stared at her, just for a moment, and then she took off, stumbling and hopping over equipment, trying not to touch any of the bodies, until she was out the front door, into the street, and gone.

"You think that was a good idea?" Mule asked. "Letting her go like that, while we're still in here?"

"I believe it will be fine," Verdino said. "I can't imagine that she's eager to turn herself in for murder."

"Stranger things have happened." Mule said. "Someone give me a hand with this bag. Eddy here is heavy."

. . .

A few minutes later, they were back in the alley. Sam and Delilah led the way, holding the door, as Sully helped Kurt and Mule with the bag that held the last remains of Eddy Santos. Professor Verdino brought up the rear, closing the morgue up carefully behind them.

"Dude," Kurt said, exasperated, "let go! You're killing us here."

"Sorry," Sully said, stepping back. "Just trying to help."

"Help someone else," Mule grumbled.

Delilah, who had taken the lead, stopped short at the street. She turned back quickly and held up her hands to stop them all.

"What is it?" Verdino asked.

"Houston?" she said, "I believe we have a problem."

Verdino stepped around her and glanced out the end of the alley. The street was bare in both directions. In the distance, they heard a siren's wail.

"Well, here we go again," Delilah said. "Looks like things are about to get Chinese-interesting again."

"Again?" Sam said. "When exactly did you get bored?"

"What do we do now?" Mule cut in. "We can't carry this guy all the way to the motel. He's freaking heavy."

"Yeah," Kurt said, "that's why we can't walk down the street with a body bag–because it's heavy. Other than that..."

Before he could finish the sentence, the Toronado screeched

around the corner with Amanda behind the wheel. She slid to a stop.

"Come on, Gregory," she said.

"The trunk," Mule said. "We have to open the trunk."

Amanda killed the engine and tossed the keys to Sam, who quickly unlocked the trunk. Kurt and Mule heaved Eddy's body up and in. Verdino, Sam, Delilah and Sully climbed into the car. Sam handed back the keys and the engine roared to life. As soon as Mule and Kurt, cursing, managed to cram themselves in, Amanda took off.

"What the hell was that all about?" Delilah asked.

"No time," Amanda said. "I'm busy. He's gaining on us."

"Who?" Sam asked.

They all turned, and at that moment bright flashing lights came to life and a siren wailed, startling them all to silence. Amanda hit the brakes, spun the wheel, and shot down a side street. Behind her the cruiser missed the turn.

THIRTY-ONE

Driving just over the speed limit, Sheriff Brogan passed a sign announcing that the Denzel exit was coming up in five miles. On a whim, he reached down and flipped through the channels on his scanner. After a moment he caught a snatch of local police traffic and left the radio on that frequency.

At first, what he heard was exactly what he expected to hear. In between random squawks and snatches of static he picked up a report of a brawl at a local tavern, a domestic violence dispute, and two change of shift notices. None of it was helpful. Then one last report came through.

"All units, we have a report of a Black Toronado eastbound near Maple and 31st. Driver is wanted for exhibition of speed and resisting arrest."

Brogan slowed and listened.

"This is Officer Brady. I got her. Holy shit! She's flying! In pursuit on West Holly"

"This is Dispatch. All units report. I repeat, all units report."

Headlights split the night and Brogan glanced up at his rearview. It was Goodman, who'd been lagging behind a bit. Brogan flipped his lights on, just for a second, sending a loud, resonant "whoop" into the night. He put on his signal to get Goodman's attention, then, as they approached the exit ramp for Denzel, he turned off and headed for town.

He flipped the radio back to the channel he'd been on just in time to catch Goodman's call.

"Brogan, where you going? You after coffee, or just need to take a leak?"

"I think we have 'em. Heard a report on police band of a Black Toronado going a little faster than the locals care for. How many of those you reckon are on the road, in this area, tonight?"

"Not many. Not more than one, probably."

"That's what I think. Let's put an end to this."

He sped up slightly, studying the signs, and turned right at the end of the ramp toward town. Goodman fell in behind and kept pace.

THIRTY-TWO

Amanda wheeled the Toronado around a corner, skidded just slightly, compensated, and floored it. They shot down the dark road so fast that the scenery on either side became nothing more than a chiaroscuro blur. The others, crammed in, half on top of one another and cramped, hung on for dear life.

"What the hell did you do?" Sam asked. "I mean, you were parked. Why are they chasing you?

"Technically, Cowboy," Delilah cut in, "I think they are now chasing *us*. And there's a dead body in the trunk. I told you it was about to get interesting."

"I'm sorry, Gregory," Amanda said. "I got bored. I just wanted to hear the engine; you know how I like V8s. I took a ride–just a couple of blocks."

"They don't turn on the lights and whoop at you for driving around the block." Delilah said.

"Well, no," Amanda said. She was grinning. "I might have been going a little fast..."

"We've talked about this, darling," Verdino chided. "There are times for exhibitions..."

"Hey prof," Kurt cut in. "Maybe it's just me, but right now doesn't seem the best time for a lecture. If you distract her, we're going right up the rear end of someone's minivan."

"Of course, of course you're right," Verdino said.

"Hold on," Amanda said. "We're heading out of town. While I was bored, I also checked the GPS on my phone. There's a side road that leads back to the highway in about...fifty feet."

She slammed on the brakes, turned the wheel, and the car spun. Just as it seemed it would fishtail and whirl out of control, she let out on the clutch, and they shot down a side-road only she had seen, leaving a cloud of dust and smoke. The black and white that had been following shot past the side street, sirens wailing.

"Jesus," Mule cursed.

Sully started to laugh crazily.

"What's wrong with you?" Delilah asked, glaring at him.

"This is a whole hell of a lot better than the family reunion I was headed for," he said. "Hell, even if you *was* aliens, I'd be in."

The Toronado roared down the old dirt road. There was no sign of pursuit. They entered the highway, turned North, and sped back toward where they left the truck.

THIRTY-THREE

rogan led Goodman into town. They drove slowly, trying to take in the situation. There weren't a lot of ways out of town, but neither of them believed there was only one. Without a better understanding of the lay of the land, all they could do was keep their eyes open and hope they got lucky. Goodman, following close on Brogan's tail, glanced into his rear-view mirror.

On the freeway behind them, flying like a bat out of hell, was a black Toronado, heading north.

"Son of a bitch!" He growled.

He grabbed the microphone.

"Brogan get back here. They're on the highway and they are moving. Fast."

"Roger, get on 'em. I'll spin and be right on your tail."

Goodman whipped his wheel to the left, skidded in a crazy U-Turn, and drove straight back down the off-ramp. It was a calculated risk. If a trucker pulled off to find a place to eat, or a room for the night, he'd have to pull over and let it pass. There was no truck, though and he reached the highway in only a few moments. He rolled down through the shallow ditch that served as a median, bumped onto the pavement on the northbound side, and hit the gas. Behind him, he saw Brogan's lights come on, and the sheriff's headlights crossing the road, but he kept his eyes on the prize.

■ ■ ■

The Toronado rushed on toward the Longhorn Valley turnoff and the road back to the truck, picking up speed steadily. The speedometer hovered around 110 mph. No one had released the precarious holds they'd taken as they bumped out of town.

Kurt turned and glanced through the rear window.

"Uh oh," he said.

Amanda glanced up and saw Goodman's lights flashing in the rearview. She pushed harder on the gas.

"Better hold on, Gregory," she said.

"You can't outrun them on a straight road," Sam said. "That cruiser has an interceptor."

"You have a better idea than trying?" Amanda asked.

Delilah started laughing. "And she does it in those fabulous heels."

Amanda pressed the accelerator the last quarter inch to the floor, and the Toronado responded.

"How far is it to the turn-off to the truck?" Mule asked.

"Too far to lose them before we hit it. We could lead them out there, but then what?"

Verdino, who'd been hunkered down, talking quietly on his cell phone, flipped it shut and sat up straighter.

"Keep driving. Help is on the way, but they are about fifty miles north. If we can get a diversion, we should be able to slip off the road and back to the truck."

"Seriously?" Delilah said. "Again? I mean, I can see you calling in the cavalry once, maybe twice..."

"Mr. Stone is very serious about this project." Verdino said. "He's not going to let us fail."

"Daddy just doesn't want me getting another ticket." Amanda said. "I have a feeling this one would be harder to 'make go away.'"

"We still have a problem." Sam said. "Police cruisers are fast. And if they use their radios, which they've been surprisingly slow to do so far, we're done."

"If they were planning on calling in backup, that time has certainly passed," Verdino said. "I believe they have decided to 'take us' on their own. When was the last time you saw a Sheriff outside his jurisdiction in a high-speed chase, accompanied by a state trooper without any sort of backup showing up?"

"You have a point," Sam said, "but still, they're gaining on us."

"I suppose we'll have to sit back, hang on, and enjoy the race," Verdino said. "In the meantime, I guess I'd better let Terence know we're coming. He reached for the phone again as they raced on through the night.

THIRTY-FOUR

Terence and Helen stood beside the tarp-covered trailer leaning on a boulder and sipping cold beer. It was very quiet. Occasionally a coyote howled in the distance, but other than that the silence was deep and unbroken. Until the phone rang. Terence sighed, stared at it a moment, shook his head, and then answered.

"Yeah?"

Verdino's voice came through weak, but clear.

"We're on our way back, but I'm afraid it's going to be a bit exciting."

"Exciting? Again?"

"That trooper, and the sheriff, are both on our tail. We have what we need, and Mr. Stone has a distraction on the way. We are going to try and get out there and get under cover. Can you be ready for us?"

"Can do. See you in a bit. And Professor? See if you can leave that trooper somewhere out at your end? Never got along with them much."

"Believe me, we'll be doing our best."

Terence hung up and drained his beer. He turned to Helen and grinned.

"We're gonna have to get out the other tarp and get ready. They're coming in with a tail."

"Well, we'd better get started then."

They turned toward the truck, lifted the edge of the tarp, and disappeared beneath it.

- - -

The Toronado didn't even slow as it passed the Longhorn Valley exit. They were maintaining their lead, but not pulling away. Goodman tried to focus on their taillights, but he glanced down nervously at the near empty gas gauge on his dash. He suddenly pounded his fist on his dash and grabbed the mic on his radio.

"Brogan, you there?"

"Right behind you, boss. What's up?"

"I may have a new problem."

"Now what?"

"Gas. I was going to fill up back at Denzel. If they keep on too much longer, I'm going to have to pull out. I'm near to running on fumes."

"You want to call for backup?"

"No way. We tell anyone what we've been up to at this point, we're dog meat."

"Well, I've still got half a tank. I'm good for a while."

"How fast is that thing?"

"I haven't touched it yet."

"I'm pulling over. You stop, I'll hop in, and we'll see if we can't catch up. There's nothing but open road for a long way."

"You got it."

Goodman pulled over and cut his engine. He got well off the road, climbed out, and made sure the vehicle was locked up tight. It was going to be hard enough to explain why he'd abandoned it without it being jacked.

A moment later, Brogan screeched to a halt in the middle of the lane, and Goodman climbed in. Almost before he had the door closed, they were off in a screeching burnt rubber cloud of smoke.

...

North of the chase, a Winnebago rolled south on the opposite side of the highway. Paisano drove, and one of his men, Cliff, sat in the passenger seat.

"Check the GPS–how close?"

"Five miles and closing fast."

Paisano pulled off the road. They moved quickly, and efficiently. Cliff ran around to the back, worked a hidden latch, and dropped the back of the trailer. He rolled two dirt bikes out and parked them to the side of the road.

"Hurry!" Paisano called.

"Done."

In the distance, headlight beams cut the almost pure darkness, rising and falling gently with the road.

"Here we go, pal." Paisano said. "Great night for a ride."

A moment later, the Toronado passed like a dark shadow. Paisano climbed in, started the Winnebago, and drove it into the road. He turned off the lights and climbed down, then he and Cliff climbed onto the bikes and took off across the desert.

...

Amanda turned and glanced at Verdino, keeping her foot firmly on the accelerator. Verdino was turned, staring back through the rear window.

"What the hell… was that?" Sam asked.

"Who is that? What are they... someone drove a freaking Winnebago across the road...and parked!" Kurt said.

Ahead, of them, there was a crossroad. To the right the desert stretched out in an endless, unbroken sprawl. To the left, there were cliffs and craggy outcroppings.

"Gregory?" Amanda said.

"Left, my dear."

Amanda braked and skidded into the turn, and they shot down the side road to the left.

"Jesus Are you freaking insane?" Delilah screeched.

Sam laughed. "What's the matter darling. Too interesting for you?"

Delilah smacked him on the head, and then she was laughing too.

Verdino was studying the GPS mapping application on his phone. After a moment he glanced up and turned to Amanda.

"There are two roads off of here within twenty miles. One leads, back toward where we left the truck. We can take that, and then go off-road and out of sight."

"You don't think they're going to follow?" Sam said.

"I'd say that depends on how fast they're moving when they reach that Winnebago." Sully cut in. "That's one big fuckin' roadblock."

In the distance, they heard the sudden screech of metal on metal and a loud crashing sound.

"Sounds like they hit something," Delilah said.

"That it does," Sam said. "Question is, was it a direct hit, or did we just piss them off?"

"If it's all the same with you folks," Amanda said, "I don't believe we'll stick around to find the answer to that."

She floored it again, and they raced down the side road into the darkness.

THIRTY-FIVE

Brogan's cruiser roared down the highway. The lights were flashing, and the siren wailed. He leaned forward, keeping watch for the Toronado, hoping to catch sight of the suddenly absent taillights.

"Where in the hell are they going?" Goodman said. "They have to know there's no way to outrun us on this stretch. There's not much between here and all the places we've already seen."

"Not sure. I'd like to know what happened to that truck."

They rounded a long curve. As the road straightened out, they saw the Winnebago parked directly in front of them. There was no way to avoid it, they were already moving too fast.

"Jesus H. Frigging..."

Brogan braked hard. They hit the right front fender of the Winnebago, caromed off and fishtailed into the desert. The cruiser spun out and stopped just off the road. The siren still wailed, and the lights flashed. Goodman, who'd cracked his head on the window, lay slumped in his seat. Brogan shook his head, dazed.

He reached up, brushed a trickle of blood from his eye.

"Jesus Christ on a pogo stick." He said. "You okay, Goodman?"

Goodman raised his head slowly. His mouth was set in a grim line.

"Will this piece of shit still run?" he said.

"I think so."

"Then get 'er running and go get them. I'm staying here to try and get that thing out of the road before someone gets killed."

"You sure you're okay?" Brogan said.

"Nope," Goodman said. "Pretty sure I'm not. Not at all."

Goodman climbed out and staggered to the driver's side of the Winnebago. Brogan rolled back onto the road and took off north.

As the cruiser pulled away, skewed to one side, but still moving, Goodman climbed up into the camper trailer, got behind the wheel, and did a quick check of his wounds. All in all, it wasn't too bad. He had a hell of a lump on his forehead, and he was bleeding, but nothing seemed to be broken. One arm was kind of numb, but his fingers still gripped, and he thought he could hold on to the wheel.

He thought about just backing off the road and checking to see if he had any bars on his cell phone, then he glanced down the long, empty length of highway after Brogan, and gritted his teeth.

"To hell with it," he said. "Might as well make it a party."

He rolled the camper forward, and then back, checking the steering, and the brakes. Everything, more or less, seemed to be in working order. He made a long, looping turn and pointed the nose of the Winnebago North. He pulled out his cell phone, and smiled. Two bars. He only hoped Brogan had as good a service as he did.

= = =

Brogan cruised down the highway, searching for signs of the Toronado. His siren wailed. The lights were half blown, but what remained continued to flash.

He came to the crossroads, slowed, and stopped. He looked both ways down the road, frowning. The road on the left was gravel – on the right it seemed like nothing more than dust. He didn't see any sign that the dirt had been disturbed. With a shake of his head, he turned left.

"Christ on a stick." He muttered. "This better be right." He drove almost a mile before it occurred to him to cut the lights and siren.

...

The Toronado flew down the old gravel trail much faster than any of them were comfortable with. Amanda concentrated, but the road was straight. Barring a king-size pothole or a jutting boulder, they were safe enough, even without headlights.

"There!" Sully called out. "Did you see that?"

He pointed behind them. Sam glanced back. Very far behind them there was a flashing glitter of blue.

"They're still coming." He said.

"It's not far to the next turn, Verdino said. "If we can get about a mile down that road, we can cut across the desert. If there's nothing in our way, that is..."

"That's more ifs there than I like to hear, Professor-man," Delilah said.

"Sorry, I'm all out of surprises. If we get back to the truck, we'll take cover, and we'll ride it out. The point in our favor is that there still seems to be no backup."

"That was true before," Delilah said, "but that might have changed when Smokey the bear hit the Winnebago. Going to be a little harder to explain that when they get back to the main office."

"It's weird," Mule said, "but I don't think they care. I think it's personal now."

"It keeps the odds better," Sam said, "but it also makes them dangerous."

"Here," Verdino said. "Turn here. If we cut straight across, we should reach the truck shortly."

Amanda slowed and turned onto a small dirt trail leading off among rocky crags.

"Why slow down now?" Delilah asked.

"I thought maybe we'd be less obvious if we didn't shoot up a dust tail." Amanda said. She turned and smiled. "I like a man in uniform, but this time out, I'll pass."

"I'm afraid I misjudged you honey. I was just sure there were no lights on in there," Delilah said.

"I get that a lot. Better to have everyone think you're dumb and helpless. You get things... and you have the element of surprise. There's a break ahead, Gregory. I'm going off road."

Amanda pulled off the road and they rolled through a small valley formed by two ridges. Amanda slowly picked up speed.

Verdino pulled out his phone and dialed quickly. When it was answered, he spoke briefly.

"Terence? We're coming in. I don't think we were followed all the way, but just in case, is our cover ready?"

"You bet. Just get on over here and we'll batten things down." Terence replied.

"Very good." Verdino said. He hung up and turned to the others. "Well, now it's up to the clock, I'm afraid. That sheriff isn't going to remain lost forever. We're going to have to do something about him."

"You talking about killing him?" Sam asked.

"No," Verdino replied, "not that, but if we could divert him from the truck—send him in the wrong direction."

"Like we did with those rednecks?" Sam asked.

"Exactly."

"Rednecks?" Sully asked. "What rednecks?"

"It's a long story," Mule said. "We get through this, I'll tell you over a drink."

They fell silent, and Amanda drove carefully, but speedily on across the desert.

THIRTY-SIX

Before long, the rocks where they'd left the truck came into sight. Amanda might have missed it, so well-covered was the area, but Terence stood outside, holding up the edge of the tarp and waiting for them, and a dim red glow seeped out from beneath. Everyone piled out quickly. Mule, and Kurt wrestled the body bag out of the trunk, and then–very carefully–Amanda drove the Toronado up under the tarp alongside the truck.

Sam and Terence quickly secured the tarp, and the rest of them made their way into the trailer of the big truck.

Once inside, Kurt and Mule set to work quickly and efficiently. They cleared off the cushions on one of the benches, revealing a stainless steel frame beneath, and a pan that drained away below. They sealed the area around the table off with plastic curtains and methodically chopped the morgue attendant's body into smaller chunks for processing.

"Hurry it up boys," Verdino said. "We don't want to leave any more evidence handy than absolutely necessary if we run into any of our friends with the flashing lights."

"Believe me," Mule said, "We're working as fast as we can here."

"Despite the last few days," Delilah said, "This is quite possibly the sickest thing I have ever witnessed."

"We could open the curtains," Mule called out.

He dropped a leg into the tank. It made a wet Thunk!

"You should have been here when we had the fry cook and that old guy. It was a mess," Kurt added.

"Mort?" Delilah said. "You mean Mort? He'll be gas?"

"A close approximation," Verdino said.

"Can't be upset about that," Delilah said. "It'll be the first good that ever came from him. Not to mention it will *not* be the first gas."

"I don't know," Sam said. "There was the pie..."

"Pie?" Sully said, perking up. "There's pie? I was gonna say, it's been a long time since we ate."

"Seriously?" Sam said. "You want to eat? You're watching some guy sliced and diced, and you want pie?"

Sully shrugged. "I'm hungry."

Everyone laughed. Mule and Kurt slowly lowered the torso into the holding tank. Next they added the head. Then, opening the curtain, Mule wheeled the tank back over to the "still" and Kurt started cleaning up.

"Once the process is started," Verdino said, "we can all eat."

"Maybe you can," Delilah said, "Me? I may just need a drink."

Terence, who'd stepped outside to take a look around, climbed back into the trailer.

"All still quiet out there. You must have lost your pals..."

The WHOOP of a siren sounded, not far off.

"And then again," Sam said, "maybe not."

"Mule," Verdino said, "I think it would be a good time to get the formula flowing into that vat."

Mule released green fluid into the holding tank. The siren whoop repeated, a little further off.

"He doesn't know where we are," Sam said. "It sounds like he might just be trying to scare us out. I'd better slip out and have a look."

"Wait!" Helen called.

She reached up to a switch on the wall and flipped it. The light in the trailer dropped to a very dim red glow.

"Now."

Sam slipped quietly out into the darkness beneath the tarp, and Delilah followed, closing the door behind them.

A few moments later, hunkered down on the desert floor, Sam and Delilah watched from beneath the tarp as Brogan drove his cruiser slowly, turning a spotlight left and right. Every few hundred yards he whooped his siren. He played the light over the tarp, and then moved on. Then he stopped and rolled back.

"Uh oh." Sam muttered.

Delilah reached for the gun. Sam stopped her.

"Wait," he said.

Suddenly lights appeared from a short distance away, bouncing up and down crazily. The cruiser went into a slow turn and tracked the newcomer. Sam and Delilah slipped out, careful to stay well back in the shadows, and watched. About fifty yards away, the Winnebago came to a bumping stop. The cruiser rolled up slowly and parked beside it. Sam and Delilah slipped back into the trailer.

As quietly as possible, they opened the door and slipped back into the trailer.

"They're here. Both of them. That crazy-assed trooper drove the Winnebago out here into the desert."

"Yeah," Delilah said, "and I don't think the Sheriff thought his buddy was coming. They parked a way off. My bet is they're swapping stories."

"That might be," Sam said, "but it won't be long before the Sheriff remembers he saw something funny back this way. Then what? We kill two cops? I mean, it might sound a little out of character, there being a trail of dead men all the way back to that coffee-shop, but, in the words of rednecks everywhere, we only killed folks that *needed* killing."

"It's true," Delilah said, almost reluctantly. "Other than the pie, Mort was a bastard."

"Time for a plan," Verdino said. "We need a distraction. I think the Toronado can outrun them, but there's no way we can get the truck out of here if the two of them remain close."

"Then I have some more bad news, Gregory," Amanda said. "That car out there is almost on empty. Not sure it would even make it back to the highway."

"Well," Mule said, grinning, "How about...a field test?"

They all turned and stared at the filters and vats.

"But," Kurt said, "It's diesel."

"Not a problem," Verdino said. "I believe I can adjust the formula to burn in a standard combustion engine. It's a good thought. Still, we have to do something about the two gentlemen out there to buy some time."

"'Bout time I did something useful," Sully said. "Got any whiskey? I was just thinking–I had me some whiskey, downed a little of it, and staggered over there–I might keep 'em busy. Might tell 'em I'd seen a mysterious black car roaring over the desert. By the time they figure I'm full of shit, you could fuel that very car and send it out. If you push it out the far end of the tarp, real quiet, and then start it up a way off. You could draw them away from here."

"That's all great," Delilah said, "but what if the gas doesn't work? What if it dies and they just pull up and take whoever's driving?"

"What's the matter kitten," Sam chuckled. "You turning chicken?"

She glared at him. "What do you think? I say let's do it. You and me. We don't really have a stake in the Prof's gas, and to be honest, I'm about done chasing around with cops on my tail. I'm thinking Mexico sounds good this time of year."

She turned to Verdino. "Fire up your gas-o-matic 'Gregory'. I've got a ride to catch."

Mule reached under a bench and pulled out a half-full bottle of whiskey. He handed it to Sully.

"You sure, man?" Terence asked. "You go out there with them, you won't sell us out? I'd hate to have to run you down with the truck."

"I'm cool," Sully said. "I'm just thirsty. When they tear out after the others, I'll be back. I might not be looking to stay," he nodded at Sam, "but I'm thinking this is the most fun I've had in years. Wherever you're all heading, jail, hell, Alpha Cen-fucking-tauri, whatever. I'm in."

"Freak," Delilah said, grinning.

Sully tipped the bottle at her and headed for the door.

"Wish me luck," he said.

Then he slipped out into the night before anyone could reply.

Sully stepped around the rocks and out into the desert. He took a deep drink from the bottle, wiped his lips on his sleeve, and started toward the Winnebago, singing. He glanced over to where the Sheriff's Department cruiser was parked. It was empty and silent.

He raised his voice a bit. "Had a little drink about an hour ago and it went right to my head…"

He banged on the side of the camper with the flat of his hand

and took another deep gulp. He walked slowly toward the front of the camper, still banging with his hand, headed up toward the driver's side door. After a few more bangs the door slammed open and Goodman climbed out.

"Halt! Hold it right there," he said.

Sully lifted the bottle overhead and squinted, as if having trouble making out who was talking to him.

"Jumpy sorta feller ain't ya?" he said.

Goodman aimed his gun at Sully's chest. "Who are you?" he said.

"Me? Bob Calvin. Folks calls me Bob, or Calvin, dependin', since I got me two first names. Who're you?"

A moment later Brogan rounded the cab, gun drawn.

"What the hell are you doing out here in the middle of the desert?"

Sully eyed the bottle in his hand, then turned back to Goodman. "Drinkin'," he said.

"You see anyone else out here? A black car, maybe a truck?"

"Didn't see no truck, but I'll tell you, I did see a car. Black like the night and going like a bat out of hell. That was about two miles back. Passed me like I was standin' still. Mebbe I was."

"You didn't see which way they went?"

Sully stared at Goodman and whistled.

"What happened to you, officer? You look like you got the business end of a pit bull on your arm."

"Never mind that," Goodman said. Which way did they go?"

Sully pointed with the bottle, careful to move slowly.

"Highway's over there. Reckon that's where they headed."

"Christ," Brogan said. "They turned back around on us."

Goodman stepped forward and took the bottle from Sully. He poured a splash of whiskey over the bandage on his arm. Then, he handed Sully the remnant and turned to Brogan.

"We'll leave the camper here." He said.

"Guess that's best. Ain't ours, anyway."

"Hey," Sully said, "You fellas mind if I get on? I got two more miles to my place, and I ain't gettin' any perkier."

Both officers glared at him. Brogan was about to say something when there was a sudden roar off to the right. It was the Toronado.

"Well, I'll be goin' to hell in a hand basket," Brogan cursed. "Get a move on partner. You got anything left at all, use it to move."

Ignoring Sully, Goodman and Brogan dashed to Brogan's cruiser. Sully leaned on the Winnebago and took another drink, saluting with the bottle as the cruiser took off into the shadows.

..

In the truck, everyone was busy. Mule and Kurt were packing equipment, tying things down and readying the rolling lab for the road. After a while Terence fired up the engine and let it idle, warming it up. Amanda stood and watched while Verdino made some hurried calculations on a clipboard.

"Wrap that up and get out there with Sully," he said. To Mule and Kurt. "Help him get the tarp down and rolled. We don't want to leave any more evidence than we have to. I don't know that they will be back this way, but if they are we should leave things as clean as possible."

"Just like boy scouts," Kurt said, grinning. "We'll leave our campsite cleaner than we found it. I don't want to be here if they come back. I've had about enough of this on-the-run fun."

"Where will we go, Gregory?" Amanda asked.

"West, I think. We'll have time to finish processing, and if our new "test drivers" are as good as their word, we'll have some performance metrics to record. We make our way through Tucson and on to California, then to the lab once we're certain no one is on our tail."

Kurt and Mule climbed down from the trailer to help Sully, leaving the two of them alone.

"Do you think Daddy will be pleased, Gregory?"

"I believe so, yes. Despite our problems, things have worked out about as we'd hoped. The process works, and I believe the military will be very interested. Imagine if you were on a battlefield, out of fuel, and you could process the enemy dead to get you home."

"I guess," Amanda said. "It's all too morbid for me. I thought we were going to use waste from chicken and cattle farms."

"Oh, we are. That's the commercial version. Everyone will be able to buy it or make it themselves on their farms. That's not what we're testing. When things–shifted–both your father and I became aware of new possibilities."

"Gregory, you tell me now. Are we turning into serial killers?"

"Not at all. In fact, we haven't killed anyone. We've just been conveniently close to a number of well-deserved homicides. I certainly don't intend to make this sort of life a habit."

"Good. I miss home, and I miss the mall. I miss my cars, and most of all I miss watching the news and not knowing anyone on it..."

Mule, Kurt, and Sully climbed back in just then. As each entered, they passed the whiskey. All of them were grinning.

"I don't recall telling you two to join Sully in that bottle."

"The tarp is stowed." Kurt said. "We're ready to go. The last of the material we collected is processed. I thought–maybe–you'd lighten up for a few minutes?"

Mule handed the bottle to Verdino, who hesitated, and then took a long swallow and smiled.

"Why Gregory," Amanda said. "How...not you!"

She took the bottle from him, drank, and returned it to Sully. Just then the hatch opened, and Helen stuck her head in from the cab.

"We're ready to roll," she said.

"By all means. South, and then West. To California, surf and sun." Verdino said.

Helen eyed the bottle of whiskey and shook her head.

"You'd better save us some of that," she said. Then she closed the hatch, and a moment later the truck rolled slowly away from the rocks, trundling off south and west, and away.

THIRTY-SEVEN

Sam drove as fast as possible. Every now and then the engine backfired, and he winced.

"Sounds like the Prof's fuel isn't quite ready for prime time." Delilah said.

"It's okay," Sam said. "I think the carb needs adjusting. It's running pretty rich. I could fix it in a couple of minutes, but now's not the time to stop and try."

"You sure?" Delilah said. "It's not gonna die on us, is it?"

"Nope. It's fine."

"Good. This has all been fun, but I've spent my week on Star Trek–it's time to get a stiff drink, a soft bed, and a couple of days of rest."

"I'd go for a couple of weeks, myself. I keep thinking Quentin Tarantino was going to step out any moment now for his cameo, and the rest of the world will blow up."

Sam glanced into the rearview.

"Christ," he said. "I don't fucking believe it."

"What?"

Delilah glanced back over her shoulder.

"You have got to be kidding me."

Sam hit the gas. Brogan's cruiser was moving up fast behind. Both officers were clearly visible. What remained of the lights were flashing.

"Whoever they are," Delilah said, "they have to be crazy driving over the desert like that."

"Or really, really mad." Sam said.

"Or both."

Off in the distance, a pair of headlight beams sliced through the failing darkness.

"The road's close," Sam said.

"Yeah," but they're coming up fast," Delilah said. "You think we can outrun them?"

"Not sure. I haven't really gunned this thing with that green... whatever it is...in the tank. Not sure how she'll react."

"I guess we're about to find out," Delilah said. "I hope this is one time I can actually depend on Mort."

Sam floored it. Everything seemed fine for about a hundred yards, and then there was a very loud backfire. The engine sputtered. The Toronado slowed, but then the engine evened out.

"That's not good."

"That's it." Delilah said. "I have fucking had it!"

She kicked out suddenly and drove her foot past Sam's into the brake. They skidded. Sam fought for control, but the engine died. The cruiser came up fast from behind. Before Sam could react, Delilah had pulled the gun and was out of the car and moving.

■ ■ ■

Brogan was driving much too fast. It took him a moment to register what he was seeing–the dark-haired woman, out of the car and coming fast, gun leveled at their faces.

"Christ! She's fucking crazy!" Brogan said.

He hit the brakes and they both ducked. The cruiser bore down on Delilah. She fired twice. Both of the cruisers front tires blew, and it went into a skid, missing her by about five feet. Delilah ran after them. The cruiser's engine died. Brogan and Goodman sat stunned. Brogan reached for his gun, but Delilah was too fast. She leaned in and slammed the butt of her gun into his head. Then, almost casually, she stepped back, aimed, and fired into the cruiser.

Without another glance, she turned and ran for the Toronado. The sun was just easing over the skyline. Sam sat behind the wheel, waiting. Delilah slipped into the passenger side seat and slammed her door.

"What the hell are you waiting on Cowboy? Get this thing moving."

"But...what did you do?"

She stared at him. "How about you drive, or I'll shoot you."

Sam started the Toronado and drove. He could still see the cruiser in the rearview but couldn't see inside it in the dark. He glanced at Delilah. She looked out the window. Sam gunned it and they shot off toward the road in the distance.

THIRTY-EIGHT

They bumped slowly through a shallow ditch and up onto the highway. Sam turned south and headed toward the border. Ahead, a sign proclaimed that the wonderful, sunny country of Mexico would be beneath their tires in ten miles. Sam glanced over at Delilah.

"Come on," he said. "Did you shoot them, or not?"

"Maybe I should just keep it a secret," she said. "It might keep you on your toes. You think you're dangling on a cop killer rap, you'll be more careful."

"Am I?"

"Maybe."

"Maybe we'd better make it a couple of months to relax. I'm starting to get a serious headache."

They drove off down the road, not speeding for once, and silent.

...

Brogan's cruiser sat still and silent in the growing morning light. The lights still flashed. Both front tires were flat. Brogan sat behind the wheel, Goodman on the passenger side. The engine remained dead, and Brogan did not try to restart it.

"Holy shit," Goodman said.

"Yeah. No doubt," Brogan replied. "You okay?"

"As okay as I was, I guess. When she aimed that gun at the window, I thought..."

"Yeah," Brogan said. "I know."

Suddenly Brogan started laughing. Goodman joined in. On the dashboard, the shattered radio dangled wires and shot sparks.

"I believe, Sheriff Brogan" Goodman said, fighting for breath, "that they're going to get away."

"You think?"

The two crawled out of the car. Brogan pulled out a cell phone. He flipped it open.

"No service," he said.

"Course not. Guess we'd better start walking. It'll give us some time to figure out what the hell we're going to tell them when we get back."

The two turned toward the road and began staggering away from the broken cruiser. The lights still flashed, strobing blue against the sky.

ACKNOWLEDGMENTS

As always, a lot of the credit for these words escaping my brain and fingers onto the page goes to the love of my life, Trish, who is my first and best editor, closest friend and a power to be reckoned with. Thanks to my sons, Zach, Zane, and Will, and my daughters Stephanie and Kat for putting up with me going on and on about the stories in my head, and for helping to keep me young. And thanks to Ron at Shotgun Honey for giving this book a home.

And I would like to acknowledge all those who were a part of the strange journey this took to completion. *Closing Time at the Sunny-Side Up* began life as a joking conversation on Twitter. It became a phenomenon - was written into a screenplay - shared on the Internet, optioned by a production company, and continues it's social media-born roll toward the Mexican border.

avid Niall Wilson is a USA Today bestselling, multiple Bram Stoker Award-winning author of more than forty novels and collections. He is a former president of the Horror Writers Association and CEO and founder of Crossroad Press Publishing. His novels include This is My Blood, Deep Blue, Sins of the Flash, and many more. His most recent published works are the collection The Devil's in the Flaws & Other Dark Truths, and the novellas When you Leave I Disappear. David lives in way-out-yonder NC with his wife Patricia, 13 cats, and a chinchilla named Pook-Daddy.

ABOUT SHOTGUN HONEY

Thank you for reading *Closing Time at the Sunny-Side-Up* by David Niall Wilson.

Shotgun Honey began as a crime genre flash fiction webzine in 2011 created as a venue for new and established writers to experiment in the confines of a mere 700 words. More than a decade later, Shotgun Honey still challenges writers with that storytelling task, but also provides opportunities to expand beyond through our book imprint and has since published anthologies, collections, novellas and novels by new and emerging authors.

We hope you have enjoyed this book. That you will share your experience, review and rate this title positively on your favorite book review sites and with your social media family and friends.

Visit ShotgunHoneyBooks.com

SHOTGUN HONEY
FICTION WITH A KICK

www.ingramcontent.com/pod-product-compliance
Lightning Source LLC
Chambersburg PA
CBHW011140190726
48289CB00012B/3096